Still DECEIVING

India

Published by:

G Street Chronicles
P.O. Box 490082
College Park, GA 30349
www.gstreetchronicles.com
fans@gstreetchronicles.com

Cover Design: Hot Book Covers
www.hotbookcovers.com

Typesetting: G&S Typesetting & Ebook Conversions
info@gstypesetting.com

ISBN: 978-0-9834311-3-8
LCCN: 2011938353

Join us on Facebook, G Street Chronicles Fan Page
Follow us on Twitter, @gstrtchroni

Still DECEIVING

Acknowledgments

As always, I have to give a huge "Thank You" to the Man upstairs, because with GOD, all things are possible. Add into that hard work and dedication, and you can watch as your dreams become your reality.

Of course, my husband Michael is next on my list because he is my support system. He keeps me relaxed when I'm on the verge of stressing out, but he reminds me to stay focused at times when I allow myself to relax a little too much, and for that I am truly thankful.

I've said it before and I'll say it again: My mom, Brenda, is a true survivor, and I've learned how to do what I have to do, even in the midst of conflict and turmoil, all by watching her handle her business on a day-to-day basis. Mom, you've taught me how to play the hand I was dealt like a professional card player, and I am grateful for the knowledge you've passed my way.

A'yanna, my baby girl, I love you more than you will ever know, and it's because of you that I do my best, even on days when it feels as if life has taken its toll on me. Although you are only five years old, I know you look up to me and watch everything I do, so it's for you that I rise and grind every morning, to show you how a woman should handle her own and not depend on anyone but God to get her through.

To my siblings, La'Mari, Jason, Darielle, Tia, Lil Doe, Dejuan, Joe, and Candace, it doesn't matter to me that some of you are my sisters from another mister or brothers from another mother. I love you all to death, and that's real talk!

Next, I have to shout out someone I can't believe I forgot in my last book, my stepmother, Tonya. I love you so much, and I'm very thankful that Daddy had someone like you in his life who still loves him unconditionally, even long after he has taken his last breath.

Also, a shout-out to my cousins, Demar and James, for supporting your girl. I know 2012 will bring great things for us, and I hope your Luxury clothing line and We I.T. music label takes off, with me and my books riding shotgun!

Thank you again to my friends, Valencia, Margo, Andreah, Travontaie, and Toya, for the support. You guys are awesome.

A shout-out to my girl, Author Queen B.G. for all of your help. Together we will make it to the top!

Again, I have to thank my dad Lacy and my in-laws, Cassandra and Michael, for their love and support, along with Auntie Bunny, Auntie Erica, and Grandma Arcola for selling my books to everyone they know, even the church folks. ☺

Thank you, G Street Chronicles, for allowing me the opportunity to publish another book. Thank you book clubs and book reviewers for allowing me to network with you, and—most of all—thank you the readers for your support! Whenever I lost the energy to write another page, paragraph, or sentence, I would get an e-mail or read a review from one of you saying that you couldn't wait for Part 2, and that was what kept me going. I hope this book will be exactly what your heart desires, and if you like it, please write a review out for me.

If I have forgotten anyone, please blame it on my mind and not my heart, because your girl ain't perfect! Just add your name here ______________________________. ☺

Love Always and Forever,

India

Dedication

This book is dedicated to the memory of Thomacine Johnson.
We miss you, Grandma! Rest in Paradise!

Prologue

I

Five years ago, my world was turned upside down when my father, Lavelle Brown (a.k.a. "Lucifer") escaped from prison, where he was supposed to be serving a life sentence. I was not overjoyed with this news, nor did I experience any of the overwhelming emotions that I, a diehard Daddy's girl from the cold streets of Detroit, had always imagined I would for the years I had patiently awaited his return. Through an unlikely source, I found out that my father was no longer the man I thought I knew. I learned that he'd hired a hit man to kill my drug-addicted mother, Lena, whom he had married straight out of high school after what he thought was love at first sight. He later put a hit on my older sister Kierra, who had also become a crack-addicted dope fiend after the horrific experience of finding our mother's dead body stuffed in a box and tossed out with the trash that was waiting to be collected on pick-up day. On one of Kierra's binges, she had stolen some money from a guy that ran one of Lucifer's trap houses with the help of her lowlife boyfriend Peanut to pay off another dealer for the debt she created with him by smoking up his shit.

Instead of Kierra getting what she had coming to her, my baby sister Tori, who was only fourteen at the time, was the unlucky one to catch that bullet. She was simply in the wrong place at the wrong time, and to top things off, that son-of-a-bitch also tried to kill me. I know you probably can't believe what I'm saying. Hell, if I wasn't there myself, I probably wouldn't believe it either, but every word of it is true—and it only got worse. One of the contract killers my father hired to take us out was the love of my life, Jermaine Williams, a.k.a. "Maine." That's fucked up, ain't it!

See, it all started after Tori was killed. I felt alone because I had no one, and I felt the dope game was responsible for it, at least in some fashion. I had to do something about it, so I did what I thought was best. I took to the streets with one thing on my mind: to shut down the game one dope dealer at a time! The only way for me to work my plan was to become a major player on these mean and corrupt Detroit streets. I had an Italian connect named Frankie, whom I knew from my days working as a call girl, and he supplied me with the best product for the low-low. I operated under the alias "LB" instead of my government name, Lovely Brown, for obvious reasons. Besides, women get no love or respect in the game, and I didn't need my girly name giving me away. Whoever said "It's a man's world" sho nuff wasn't lying!

My team consisted of me; Meechie, an old-school nigga who knew his shit; my play brother, Do It; and his chick, who was also my good friend, White Girl. On top of that, we had the help of a few other niggas from 'round the way. Our shit was solid, and we were bringing in more money in one hour than some could imagine getting in their lifetime. Our days consisted of poppin' tags and livin' the good life, and our nights consisted of scratching names off our list and shuttin' shit down. Everything was everything, but not everything was gravy, because while on our mission, we ended up making enemies with the Feds for our drug empire and massive income. That wasn't a huge shocker, but it was a minor setback. At the same time, we were placed on Lucifer's shit list for being in the way when he broke out of prison, ready to reclaim his throne as king of the streets, and we also managed to piss off the mafia, who placed a million-dollar bounty on my head for some shit I didn't even do. Like I said, everything was not gravy.

When shit started getting crazy, I was ready to bounce and put Detroit in my rearview mirror, but after all my trap houses and stash houses were robbed simultaneously, I needed just one last package to make some more money to get me wherever it was I was going. I called Frankie and was sent to pick up the package from his nephew, but when I got there, the entire place was shot up, and everyone inside was dead! Somebody had set me up! They wrote "LB" on the wall in blood and stole a million dollars from the safe as well. I hauled ass to get out of Dodge, but my plan was stalled when my play brother, Do It, who was my driver and my right-hand man, went missing and White Girl went into premature labor. I couldn't leave Detroit without my people. Before I took off, I was going to find Do It no matter what, and we would snatch White Girl up and hit the road. Of course, my plan was derailed again, because right in the middle of all the chaos and confusion, I received a phone call from someone who demanded I say my last words to my brother. Not a word had left my mouth before I heard the two shots popping off on the other side of the phone, and then my phone died. Although my heart wouldn't let me believe the obvious, my mind told me my brother, a die-hard nigga that had been around me my whole life, was gone and never coming back.

Figuring that no one was safe around me, I decided to leave White girl in the hospital. I would have died if something happened to her or my little niece in the womb, who was already fighting for her life. I needed some getaway money, so I made a stop at my office because I was sure I had a nice stash of cash in my floor safe; as luck would have it, I was right. I loaded the duffel bag like a mad woman and was caught off guard by my sister Kierra, who I almost shot, thinking that she was an intruder. Earlier that day, I had seen her down at the hospital while I was visiting White Girl. She said she had something important to tell me that just couldn't wait, so I told her to meet me in the office. In all the melee, I guess I had forgotten that.

She ended up confessing to me that she led those killers to my house, but she swore it was not on purpose. She said she had hit a lick and wanted to do something nice for Tori, so she broke into my apartment put money on Tori's bed, then slipped out quickly. She didn't know she was being followed by the men who were hired to take her life—a result of that same lick she had just hit. The men waited inside my apartment, ready to do some damage, thinking Kierra would return shortly—but I don't have to tell you how that story ended.

She told me that after I disowned her and blamed her for the death of Tori, she immediately checked into rehab. She wanted to turn her life around, but it was too late, because she was soon diagnosed with AIDS. God only knew what my sister was going through, and I wanted to stay there and consoler her, but if I didn't leave right away, we would both be dead. So I gave her some money for her medicine and told her I had to go. I also warned her to stay away from our father since he was the madman behind the whole nightmare. Right on cue, I noticed on the surveillance monitors from the cameras outside that we were no longer alone. About fifteen masked men surrounded the place, with their guns in hand, I knew it wasn't good at all. I grabbed my sister's hand, and we headed down into the basement. A few days after we bought the place, I'd had a tunnel built down there for emergencies just like that one. As she helped me move boxes from the wall, she asked what it was, and I told her it was a secret passageway with two paths. One led straight to the getaway car in the driveway, and the other was a ladder that would take us to the alley.

Kierra took the way to the car, prepared to throw them off so I could escape, even though I begged and pleaded with her not to. "Keep going, Lovely. My life ends here. One sister died because of me already, but this time, one sister will live because of me." We exchanged "I love you's" while I climbed the ladder to the alley, and in seconds, she was in the car, ready to save my life.

It looked and sounded like being on Jefferson for the annual fireworks display when they shot up my sister, killing her instantly. Although I was unbearably sick to my stomach, I knew there was no reason to stop and turn around. Going back would have been useless, because there was nothing to go back to. My big sister was gone, and once they realized it was her instead of me, the man hunt—or the woman hunt, for that matter—would begin.

I ran as fast as I could through the alley, jumping over trash and dodging stray cats. I made it to a main street just as a city bus approached, and I was thankful for that. Finally feeling safe and secure, I didn't think twice about getting on. I dropped my duffel bag and caught my breath, and then I paid the driver a stack to take me as far as he could go without stopping. Just then, I turned around and saw a face I recognized. It was Lucifer himself, dressed as a homeless man. He applauded me for a job well done.

Without hesitating or skipping a beat, I went for my piece just as he went for his. When our guns were pointed at each other and I was about to blow his muthafuckin' head off, he started talking shit, trying to mess with my mind. "Baby girl, don't you miss Daddy?" When I had nothing to say, he continued, "Lovely, they had to go. They were liabilities," he answered, reading my mind. I still didn't say one word, so he went on, "Your mother was a fucking crack head, and you know I don't condone that shit. She was sucking and fucking every nigga or bitch with a dollar. Her ass was dirty and disrespectful, and everybody knew she was my wife." He pointed to himself, and I caught a glimpse of a bezel diamond pinky ring and Rolex watch. I cursed myself out in my head because had I been on my game, I would've noticed that shit and the brown Gucci loafers he was wearing under the dingy get up when I first stepped on the bus. If I would've been paying attention, maybe my ass would've gotten right off that damn bus. "She was supposed to hold it down until I came back for her, but she fucked that up in the most disrespectful way, Lovely. She had to go!" he barked and then took a step toward me.

"Forget Lena! You right. She was a junkie, not to mention a

poor excuse for a mother." I gave him no grief about my mother because it was no secret that she was not my favorite parent. When I was younger, there were so many days when I went hungry and many nights when I went to bed dirty because of lack of running water. My father had given her a huge amount of money to hold us over, but the only people to see most of it were drug dealers. "But just tell me one thing…why would you kill your own flesh and blood, your baby girl, Tori? She was just a kid, and she never did nothing wrong to nobody! She had her whole life ahead of her," I said, holding back the tears as I thought about how much I loved my fourteen-year-old sister and how she was so much like my baby. I was only five years older than Tori, but she was indeed like a daughter. I was too young to be her mother, of course, but I would've done anything to make sure she was happy and well taken care of.

"Tori was in the wrong place at the wrong time. Those bullets were meant for Kierra, and I'm sure you know that by now," he said without a shred of remorse, like *"Oops! It was an accident, but what's done is done."*

"Shit! Kierra was your blood too. Hell, she was your firstborn!" I snapped.

"Muthafucka, *I'm* your blood, and you standing here with a gun pointed at me like I'm a nigga in the street," I said, pointing out the obvious.

"Lovely, the day Kierra became a crack head was the day I disowned her as my daughter, and she fucking robbed my guy, so you know she had to pay. Family is family, but baby, business is business—and it don't matter who you are. She put herself in a fucked-up situation, and she knew the consequences. Junkie, prostitute, dealer, worker, lookout, narc, judge, or lawyer—when you play in these streets, you got an expiration date. Baby, that girl's time was up, and that's just the way it is! As for you, LB—that's what they callin' you these days, right?"

He looked up at me with a smile that could melt hearts and the most beautiful emerald-green eyes that always seemed to amaze me. When I was younger I used to love to stare into them because they were the exact shade as mine. I always thought my father looked a lot like actor Terrance Howard and was perfect and could do no wrong. So, it puzzled me when people in the media downed him, calling him names like "murderer" or "monster" or "the Devil." It angered me, and I couldn't understand why so many people said those untrue things about my daddy. Every night, I prayed that people would see the beautiful, kindhearted, giving man who tucked me and my sisters in bed, smothering us with Eskimo kisses and telling us bedtime stories. However, standing there on that bus looking his cold-hearted ass in the face, I could've sworn he had horns coming out of his head and a pitchfork in his hand, but the more I stared at it, the more reality told me it was really just a Desert Eagle aimed right between my eyes.

"Well, as for you, it's simple, baby. I'm home now, ready to reclaim my position as GOD on these streets." He raised his arms up like he was the king of kings and the lord of lords. "Unfortunately, I can't do that with you in my way. You got the connect straight from the muthafuckin' MOB, and I want it!" he said through clenched teeth.

"How do you know about my connect?" I asked, as it all began to make sense. I knew I had been set up, but I didn't know who had done it, so when Lucifer told me he knew about my connect, I had my culprit.

"I run this shit, Lovely, and don't you ever forget that! I been keeping tabs on you since the first day you entered the game, baby. I knew about Maine and how much he loved you, even if you didn't know he killed your mom and was there when your sister was killed. I know about Do It and White Girl's baby. Don't shit go down in the 'hood without me knowing about it!" he barked.

"So you mean Maine isn't working for you anymore?" I asked with a confused look on my face. Maine and I had been dating for a while, but we never really disclosed our line of business with each other. He didn't know I was the notorious drug dealer LB, and I didn't know he was the contract killer hired to take my empire down. He had tried to warn me about my father just hours earlier, but I thought he was out to get me, so I fled from the hotel we were hiding out in. From the looks of things, I should've stayed my ass with him, and maybe I wouldn't have found myself in that position on that bus. "You set me up with my connect, and you put the Feds on me, too, didn't you? You bastard!" I continued.

"I may be a lot of things, baby, but you know damn well I ain't no fucking snitch. After all, I got knocked because some snitch-ass nigga couldn't keep his fucking mouth closed. So to answer your question and make it clear, no. You got the Feds on your ass all by yourself, baby girl. You was running major weight and clocking dollars, and if you caught everybody's attention in Detroit, then you know you caught their attention. The Feds see everything." He glanced down at his fancy watch. "Anyway, I'm glad we had this little chat, but it looks like our ride has come to an end," he said, taking a step closer to me.

I stepped back. "Don't fucking come any closer to me, or I'm going to blow your fucking brains out!" I yelled.

He stepped closer to me again, and again I stepped back. "Baby girl you ain't no real killer, because if you was, you wouldn't have warned me. You would've just pulled that trigger," he said, taking another step toward me and putting his hand over my gun.

I backed up but bumped right into the bus driver. He hemmed me up into a full nelson, causing me to drop my gun. "What you want me to do with her, boss?" he asked, as the bus crept along.

I could've kicked myself. I hadn't even noticed that the bus was barely moving. I looked up at his six-seven frame and noticed a huge slash scar across his entire face, starting from under his chin and ending right at his temple. I wished I had a machete so I could put another one on the other side to make an X. That bastard who had a hold on me needed crossing out. My hopeful gaze once again fell upon my father's menacing scowl, as I waited for him to answer his goon, but I knew for certain that my life was over. There was no need to scream. It was two o'clock in the morning, and no one was out except bums, dope boys, and crack addicts, who were not about to play Captain Save-a-Ho for my ass.

"Lovely, I'm sorry it has to end like this, but it is what it is—no hard feelings." He brushed a piece of dangling hair away from my face and then planted a kiss on my cheek like some type of bullshit straight out of the movies. "Tell your mother and sister I said hello." He put the barrel of his gun right up against my forehead, and I didn't even flinch or close my eyes because I wasn't going to give his sorry ass the satisfaction. There was no point in begging him to spare my life because I knew my father wasn't cut out like that. In all the years I'd known him, he'd never changed his mind about anything. Once he said it, it was done!

II

To my surprise, I heard a *CRASH* instead of a gunshot. The bus spiraled out of control and did two flips across the street and finally rested upside down, on its roof. I flew into the seats and hit my head on a window or two in the commotion. I must've been unconscious for more than a few minutes, because when I came to, I heard the police sirens blaring in the distance and saw my father and his big-ass bus driver goon hopping out a window in the back of the bus and disappearing into the night air. "Shit!" I said as I put my hand to my head, which was now bleeding. I stood on shaky legs and stumbled for a few steps, and then I heard *BANG* behind me and someone calling my name. I turned toward the huge windshield in the front of the bus and saw that it was Maine.

"Hold on, baby! I'm coming!" he said as he kicked the cracked windshield several times until it finally caved in.

Even with all that was going on, I wasn't about to leave money behind, so I reached for my duffel bag before I took his hand and let him help me climb out the window. We ran across the street and jumped into the cab of an eighteen-wheeler that his ass had to have stolen.

"You okay?" he asked, checking out my head.

"Yeah. Just go! I heard sirens," I said, knowing it was best to elude the police. I knew the FBI was still looking for me, and I wasn't trying to make their search any easier.

"Baby, I'm glad you're okay. I told you that nigga was crazy!" Maine looked over at me with a look that said, *"I told you so, but yo'ass didn't want to listen."*

"Yeah, he is, and I'm glad you came to my rescue. I'm so sorry for not believing you when you said you honestly didn't know who I was and..." I trailed off because I got choked up and began to cry. It was not like me to shed a tear, but the stress of the day was really starting to get to me.

"Baby, your head is gushing blood. We need to get to a hospital," he said, obviously concerned.

"No! No hospitals for me," I said. I instantly remembered that White Girl had been checked in there earlier when her water broke, and I debated on leaving her there because I thought she would be safer without me. But now that my father had mentioned her and her pregnancy, that shit concerned me—not to mention the last thing I promised my brother before he went missing was that I would get back to the hospital and make sure they were okay. Fucked-up situation or not, I was a woman of my word. "Wait... scratch that! Get me to the hospital. I need to get White Girl before my father does," I said as fear gripped my heart. Even though I knew going there wasn't the smart thing to do because the cops would probably be looking for me, I just couldn't lose another person I cared about. It didn't matter if I came out dead, alive, or in handcuffs. The shit was about to go down. "You got guns in here?" I asked. I'd left my piece behind in the bus debris, even though I managed to grab my duffel bag with the money in it.

"Yeah, I got three," Maine said. He handed me a black Glock .40.

"What kind of hit man only has three guns?" I quizzed as I wiped my bloody hand across my jeans that were already bloody from earlier, when I had rushed White Girl to the hospital.

"One who stole this truck from the hotel parking lot to look for his girl after she left. I thought we'd just keep riding. I didn't know we had to go bust somebody out of the hospital." He licked his lips; he still looked sexy, even under pressure. My man was fine, and he was a cold-blooded killer. In my book, that shit was double my pleasure. In that moment especially, I was so thankful to have him on the team and to know he had my back.

We pulled up to the main entrance of the hospital. With no time to waste, I flew through the double doors like a gust of wind. I placed the gun in my jeans and tried my best to look normal, but there was blood pouring from my head, and everyone was looking at me.

"Ma'am, are you all right? Do you need to see a doctor?" asked the old receptionist with a wig straight from the sixties, just as the elevator opened.

I didn't respond or even offer her any eye contact. I just flew inside with Maine in tow and pressed the button to close the door, almost before she got the questions out.

"Shit! You know they gon' send security up there, right?" he said, looking down at me.

I looked up at him and just shrugged my shoulders. I was prepared for anything, and I had come too far to stop. "At this point, baby, it is what it is," I replied. I pulled my gun out and stepped off the elevator with one thing in mind: I had to locate and retrieve what the fuck I came for. I looked down the hall. I didn't see any of the security I had hired to sit outside of White Girl's door, and a red flag went up. It was not a good sign. I tried to peer through the small square window on the door before I entered, but the curtain was closed, so I tapped lightly. When I didn't get a response, I pushed it open with force. "Candace? You in here?" I said, calling out her government name.

The curtain swung back, and both Maine and I pointed our guns in that direction. "Please let my patient…OH MY!" A black lady doctor jumped back and dropped the clipboard she was holding with a loud *CLANG*!

"Shhh," I said as I went over and gently shook White Girl, who was still sleeping.

"Lovely, did you find Do It?" She looked up at me with a panicked expression.

Not knowing what to say or how to say it, I lied. "Yeah, boo. He's downstairs waiting for us back at the car, so we need to go. Okay?" I helped her sit up.

"She can't leave or the baby will come too soon," the doctor pleaded.

"Look, Doc, I need you to unhook her now. This is an emergency—a life or death situation. She is not safe here. Her life is in danger, and I have to get her out of here right now," said Maine.

Without asking any more questions, the doctor went to work unplugging all the machines. I slid the hospital-provided cloth house shoes on White Girl's feet, and when the doctor noticed her shaking, she took off her lab coat and put it across her shoulders.

I peeked into the hallway. So far, the coast was clear, so we made our way to the elevator.

"They have cameras in there. They are going to see us coming," Maine said.

I knew it was our only option since we were on the fifth floor. "Well, you can't carry her down all those stairs, can you?" I asked as we looked at the doctor, who tried to turn and walk away casually. "Please, Doc. You're the only chance we have to get out of here," I begged.

"We won't hurt you," Maine added for good measure.

She stopped and stared at us for a brief second, probably contemplating her options of helping us or turning her back on us and running the risk of being shot. Moments later, she moved toward us, but her ass wasn't moving fast enough, and I was the bitch with the gun, so I snatched her ass up, put the gun to her head, and pushed her into the elevator that had just arrived.

Seconds felt like hours as we waited for the elevator to reach the main level, and the anticipation had me clutching the trigger tighter than a mutha. The minute the elevators doors swung open, I wished I was anywhere else.

"Please step out with your hands up!" was what I heard before I saw all of Detroit's finest in blue with their guns drawn, pointed right at us.

I looked at Maine. *It's now or never*, I thought.

"Hey! We have two hostages, so don't shoot. I have a pregnant patient and a doctor!" he yelled.

I wrapped my arm around the doctor's neck and held my gun to her head, and Maine did the same with White Girl. There was also a gang of alphabet agents in the crowd with their pistols pointed at us. It was a real party.

"I swear to God I will kill this bitch if you don't back the fuck up!" I screamed. I didn't really want to shoot the doctor, but desperate times called for desperate measures.

"Please release your hostages, or we are prepared to shoot in ten…nine…eight…"

Fuck! What am I going to do now?

"Seven…six…five…four…"

POP! POP! POP!

I let off my gun after Maine let off his. He must've given White Girl the third gun, because she was popping rounds too. Hurriedly, we backed our way into a stairwell that wasn't too far from where we were standing and wasn't blocked by the cops. Once the door was closed, Maine put White girl on his back, and she hung on for dear life. I let the doctor go, and we flew down the stairs. Bullets ripped through the metal door, leaving dents, dings, and holes with jagged edges.

When we made it to the bottom, I noticed that the doctor was right behind us, and I looked at her like she was crazy. "Doc, you're free go the other way."

"Follow me," she said.

Not bothering to ask why, we did as we were told. She led us to an underground tunnel that hospital staff used to transport patients from one hospital to another without having to go outside. I was elated to discover that most of the hospitals in downtown Detroit were so close and connected by the tunnel.

"Now, just go through that door, and you'll end up inside of children's hospital. Take the service elevator to the lobby, and it will put you down the street from this hospital, away from those cops. Hurry, though. They might know about this tunnel too," she warned.

I nodded my thanks and appreciation with a smile.

Needless to say, Heaven must've been on our side, because we made it out unscathed. Nobody was on the other side waiting for us, and I was geeked because truthfully, with my head injury and other wounds, I was beginning to feel as if I would lose the battle for lack of energy.

At Maine's direction, we caught one of the cabs that was waiting curbside to assist patients. He directed the cabbie to take us to some secret house he'd been keeping up in Ann Arbor for just such an emergency. Our plan was to escape the next morning and head far, far, far away from there, but as fate would have it, my niece, DeShawna Tori Wright, was born that very night. *I swear, if it wasn't for bad luck, I wouldn't have any luck at all.* At five pounds, eight ounces, she was a tiny newborn, but she was beautiful—the spitting image of her dad. The moment for me was bittersweet: bitter because my brother couldn't be there to see his creation come into the world, but sweet because I managed to keep my word by getting them out of harm's way. That beautiful little angel was proof that going back was the right thing to do.

Not only did DeShawna have her father's features, but my little niece also had her daddy's strength. With only her Auntie Lovely and her Uncle Maine to help her come into the world—no doctors or nurses or incubators—she still survived without any complications, just like a normal forty-week baby. Of course, after the labor and delivery and things had calmed down, White Girl asked again where her man was, and I had to explain to her that

Do It wasn't coming home. Even after all we'd been through and survived, hearing that news broke her and just about killed her.

* * *

Things were rocky for the first few weeks. White Girl barely touched DeShawna, and I knew it wasn't because she was a bad mom. No, it was because she was hurt! Who wouldn't be? She couldn't believe the love of her life was gone, and to be honest, neither could I. Do It was the type of person you expected to last forever, and the fact he didn't really had me fucked up, too, but life had to go on, and that baby needed me and my attention. All that other shit was tossed on the back burner.

The "safe house," as I called it, was sort of like a mini mansion, with six bedrooms, eight bathrooms, a huge kitchen, a media room, a swimming pool, a bar, and even a billiards room. We never had to leave for nothing if we didn't want to because Maine had saved a lot of money from his killing days. We could pay anybody to go out and buy or do shit for us in total confidence. We debated about getting out of Michigan as soon as Shawnie was a little stronger and able to travel. With Maine's money, we could've gone anywhere we wanted in the whole damn world, but in the end, we ended up staying right where we were . We figured by the time we left, every highway and bi way would be swarming with people trying to find us.

Maine said the smart thing to do would be to just chill out and post up, because nobody would ever think to look for us there. Much to my surprise, he was right, and nobody ever did. Believe it or not, we held it down for five years with no Feds, no Lucifer, no mafia, and no problems. Then one morning, much to my dismay, I woke up with the feeling that shit was about to get real and hit the fan *again*. This time, though, I would be ready, and you could bet your bottom dollar I wasn't about to back down. I was going out with guns blazing, even if I lost my life in the process, and you can believe that!

Present Day

CHAPTER 1

"Auntie L, how come we have so many locks on the door?" DeShawna asked me as we walked inside the house.

Every time I picked her up from the bus stop, which was about ten steps from our front door on the cul de sac we lived in, she asked me the same question, and everyday I gave her the same answer: "Because, Shawnie, we have to keep the bad people out."

She sat her Dora the Explorer book bag down by the front door and frowned.

"What's the matter?" I asked.

"Well, I was wondering why bad people would want to get into our house?" She looked up at me with her big brown eyes, and I seriously thought about how I would answer that question, 'cause it was a new one.

Just as I opened my mouth to speak, I was saved by the bell when Maine walked into the house. Right on cue, he answered the question for me. "It's just for safety, baby. No one wants to get in our house, so you don't have to worry about that. Okay?" He kissed me on the cheek and smiled at DeShawna.

"Okay, but are you sure? Auntie L has a trillion-million-zillion locks on the door. Plus, we have the alarm thingy, and if we go out, Mommy always takes a different way home every time."

I looked at her in amazement. The five-year-old was too damn observant for me. "I'm sure, Shawnie. Auntie L only has a zillion locks because I'm just being super safe, and your mommy too. Now go change into your play clothes. Okay?" I said.

She did as she was told.

I turned to Maine and wrapped my arms around his waist. "I missed you, baby." He had only been gone for about two hours, but that was still too long to be without my chocolate thug. He still handled business from time to time because he was not the type of nigga to relax and chill while there was things to do and more money to be made. That was just the kind of person he was, and I knew there was no changing it, so I never saw a reason to put up a fuss—as long as he retuned home in one piece, and he always did.

"I missed you, too, baby. So when are you going to give me one of those?" he said, looking down at me.

"Give you one of what?"

"An inquisitive five-year-old," he said, never removing his gaze.

"Baby, we'll have one of our own one day, but we aren't even married yet?" I said and then instantly regretted bringing up that fact. He had asked me several times to marry him, but I kept putting it off. I didn't want to leave a paper trail with our names and address on it for every killer in Detroit to find once it became public record. Maine thought everything was over, but I knew better. I was just too paranoid for my own good, and I was waiting for something to shake up our somewhat normal world. He and White Girl kept reminding me that it had been a whole five years and I should relax, but I just couldn't. I knew life would never be the same for me again. I was always waiting for something to happen or for someone to pop out of a closet or something. I knew that was getting old for them, but that was the way I felt, and there was nothing anybody could say or do to change that.

"You're right. We ain't married, but that's because of you, and

I don't understand why, Lovely," he said, pushing away from my hug.

I knew I had struck a nerve, and I was mad at my-damn-self for even going there in the first damn place. "Baby, don't start with me. You know the deal. We can't be on paper…that marriage shit is public record," I explained, trying to fix my mess.

"Whatever, Lovely! I mean, shit, let's go to a different state and do it then—hell, another fucking country!" he snapped, calling my bluff.

"You know I don't travel any—"

"That's the fucking problem," he said, cutting me off. "You don't do shit anymore. We don't leave Ann Arbor. You got everybody in this bitch paranoid—even the baby—and I'm tired of it!" he said and began to walk away. I grabbed at his arm, catching him by the sleeve of his Ralph Lauren button-up. "Baby, don't walk away. I'm sorry. I love you and you love me, so I don't know why we need that piece of paper to tell us that."

He looked down at my hand like I had no right to be touching him, and then he said, "It ain't 'bout the paper, but without it you won't give me a baby, right?"

Damn that nigga got me again. "Maine, a damn marriage license isn't really the reason I won't have a baby. To tell the truth, I'm scared to death that someone will find out about him or her. If that happens, not only do I have look over my shoulder for the rest of my life to watch my own ass, but then I'll have to do that for someone else," I said.

He didn't speak. He just gave a knowing smile kissed me on my head and walked up the stairs.

I hated moments like that, and the fact that we didn't really have any other outlets or places to go except for another room in the house or the backyard made it all the more awkward. It's hard to avoid speaking to someone when they're in the same house. Although the house was pretty big, over the years, it had become really small in moments like those.

Over the past five years, we'd had the same debate several times, and I knew he was growing tired of the same old song and dance. He had only stayed for so long because he loved me, but I have to admit I was constantly wondering when love wouldn't be enough to continue the fight in life with me. Without Maine, I wouldn't have been able to keep it together for so long, partially because his money kept us comfortable and job free. He'd saved up millions during his time as a hit man for my dad and other street employers. He'd gotten in the game young and turned killing-for-pay into a very lucrative business. Through his private connects, he was also able to find out what was going down in the streets; that kept us light on our feet and quick on our toes, steps ahead of anybody who might have been looking for us. But I was still paranoid anyway.

I saw White Girl coming in form the backyard, closing the patio door behind her. I knew she had just finished smoking a cigarette, not only because I could smell it, but also because it had become the norm for her. She was constantly puffing on a Newport and sipping anything with liquor in it. Over the past five years, I'd watched her change, and not really in a good way. Don't get me wrong: She was still my girl, and I loved her like a sister, but I could tell that life was taking its toll on her. She was still hurt and dealing with the loss of Do It, and that was to be expected, but I think she would've been a little better off if she didn't have Shawnie—her daddy's twin—as a constant reminder of what she had lost. Her life was missing the love of her man, and I felt bad for her. "Wassup, L?" She asked.

"Nothing much. Just the same-old-same-old with Maine," I said, checking the mail I had been holding in my hand since I walked inside with Shawnie. I knew it was only junk mail like catalogues and magazines because none of us ever had serious mail come to the house in our names; we used P.O. boxes to cover our tracks.

"Girl, you need to get up off it and give that man a baby," she said, smacking her lips. She had been siding with him since the beginning on the issue. She went to the refrigerator and grabbed a can of Heineken, popped the top with her teeth, and took a huge gulp in one swift motion.

"Well, damn! Am I the only one concerned about Lucifer and Frankie—not to mention the Feds?" I tore up the junk mail and placed it in the trash as I sat down on the kitchen stool across from the sink where she was standing.

"Girl, you need to stop worrying about what *might* happen and just take a chance on love. Nigga's like Maine and Do It don't last forever," she said and then got choked up.

I went over to her side and wiped her face. "Girl, it will be okay. I know it's hard, but we will get through this together, I promise. It don't even seem like it's been five years since we lost him, Kierra, and Tori, but we've made it this far, and every day it seems to get a little easier," I consoled, wiping my own tears away. I thought about the people I'd lost all the time, and it killed me not have my family with me, but that's life: people die. We don't want it to happen, but for real, there are some things we just can't change. We cried silently together for a few minutes, just as we did from time to time on their birthdays or Christmas.

A few seconds later, we heard DeShawna making her way down the steps, taking them one at a time. We broke our embrace and wiped our tears like nothing happened. My niece knew her daddy was in a better place because that was what we'd told her, but she was still too young to understand the seriousness of the situation, and I knew that if she saw us upset or crying, she'd start too, and I didn't want that.

"Auntie L, are you going to watch *Dora* with me?" she asked as she entered the kitchen and stood next to me.

"Don't I always?" was my reply. Me and Shawnie were tight, and I loved that little girl to pieces. In some ways, I was like her mother because I picked up White Girl's slack when she wasn't emotionally able to be there for her baby. I did movie nights in the media room with pajamas and popcorn. I did baths and stories at bedtime. I also did a lot of visits at school, not only to be active with her and her teachers, but also to protect her and be there just in case anything ever went wrong. I didn't even want her to go to school in the first place, but Maine and White Girl pleaded with me, saying it would be unhealthy and not beneficial for her to be home-schooled. After much thought and consideration, I finally gave in—not just because I thought they had a point, but also because White Girl was her mother. Ultimately, the choice was hers.

CHAPTER 2

Just as Shawnie and I were about to make our way into the fourth bedroom, which we had turned into her playroom, my doorbell rang, I headed back downstairs and peered through the peephole. I smiled because it was my best friend in the world, Coco. "How in the hell did you get past the gate?" I half-joked with my girl as I let her inside.

"You know that goofy-ass security guard like me and always lets me right in." She hugged me tight.

"I'm going to have to get them to fire his ass," I said, and I meant it. Yeah, Coco was my bitch till the world blew, and I knew she would never blow up my spot to anybody, but that dumb-ass rent-a-cop was known to let anything with a big butt and smile inside of this community. That shit wasn't cool, especially for someone like me. I had plenty of enemies.

"Wassup, little mama?" Coco greeted Shawnie.

"Hi," was all she said in return and then hid behind me, clutching my thigh for dear life.

"Shawnie, it's okay. This is my very best friend in the world. Her name is Coco, and she won't hurt you," I leaned down and told her.

Coco was the only person in the world who knew where I lived, and she had only been there to visit about four times in all the years

I'd been gone. For the first year, we only kept in touch through bogus minute-long phones, and my code name when we talked was "Leslie." We thought people were watching her because she knew me, and we didn't want her to be followed, so the phones were all we had to keep in touch. But halfway through the second year, I was really missing my girl, so I was willing to take the chance and let her visit. She would come out on weekends, and we would just kick back and reminisce about the old days.

"Auntie L, are you still going to play with me?" Shawnie asked.

"Yes, baby, I will, but can I play later?" I hated to break my niece's heart, but it had slipped my mind that this was the weekend Coco was coming.

"Okay…I guess." She hunched her shoulders and ran off, calling to her Uncle Maine to play Barbies with her.

Coco and I laughed.

"Damn, bitch. Yo' ass is getting fat," she said, poking at my stomach.

I looked myself over in the mirror hanging on the wall. *Fat? No. Thick? Most definitely!* "Shut up, nigga. I went from a five to a seven, and I think it looks good on me. Check you out. You got a new look too." I pointed to the short red hairdo she was sporting. Anybody who knew Coco knew that long weave with wild-ass colors was her signature look, so I was a bit taken aback with her new hairstyle. She was damn near bald, like the way rapper Eve used to wear hers when she first came out. Now, don't get me wrong: It looked nice, and it did complement her face, but it was way beyond the norm for the old Coco. My girl was a bona fide ghetto girl, straight from the Brewster housing projects, and she loved every minute of it. She could fry dye and lay some hair, so when I started opening up front businesses with my dope money, she was the first person I helped. Her salon was called Salon 3k. She said she named it that "because it's a millennium ahead of the competition," and she was right. Everybody loved Coco's skills, and sometimes her townhouse in the projects was filled to capacity with people of all ages and races, lined up for one of her creations.

"Yeah, girl. Shit, with all them damn clients I got, it's hard as hell to keep my own hair straight. This cut is cute and practical." She finger-swept it as she looked in the mirror.

"Come on. Let's put your bags up." I walked up the stairs and turned toward the fifth bedroom in the east wing of the house, next to my room. Shawnie's bedroom, playroom and White Girl's bedroom were all in the west wing.

As we passed my room, Maine was sitting there on the floor playing dolls with Shawnie. I cracked up laughing at his big ass looking so out of place.

"What y'all laughing at?" He stood up and gave Coco a hug.

"Bro, you too damn big to be playing wit' dolls," Coco teased, and Maine had to laugh at himself. I was glad the two of them were cool, because up until we left Detroit, they really hadn't had too much contact—just brief interactions with each other here and there.

"Where are my lil niggas?" Maine asked about her two sons, Corey and Cordell, my godsons.

"They too damn old now, and they talk too much, so they had to stay behind. If they would've come, this secret wouldn't have been a secret for long."

She was right, but I did miss them. The first and only time they came was on Coco's first visit. The were about six and four years old at the time, but now they were nine and seven, talking like nobody's business.

"Fo' sho! I understand, but if you ladies don't mind, I have some important business I need to tend to." He nodded at Shawnie, who was now pulling at his shirt from behind. We laughed again and went into the guest room.

"Maine ass is still fine. Damn!" she burst out.

I smiled.

"Girl, that nigga is the total package. He fine, he got a body like I ain't never seen, he paid, and he a hood nigga. That's the shit champions are made of right there!" She gave me a five.

"Girl, you are stupid." I sat down on the plush Cali King bed and lay across it while I watched her unpack her things and hang them up.

"Girl, bye! You know that nigga is the shit. Do he got a brother?" She looked back at me with a bitch-I'm-dead-ass-serious look on her face.

"Look at you! Now didn't you just tell me on the phone the other day that the nigga you been messing with for three years just popped the question?" I quizzed.

"Yeah but a bitch didn't say 'yes,' yet, so ain't shit wrong with asking if yo' rich-ass, fine-ass nigga got a rich-ass, fine-ass brother!" She laughed, and so did I. Her ass was definitely not the wife type. All her life, she played nigga after nigga and still fucked with her baby daddy, Zo, at the same time.

"Why you ain't say 'yes'?" I asked, and she looked at me all serious.

"Because, L, you wouldn't be there for my wedding, and you know I ain't having none of that." She sat down on the beige leather recliner on the side of the bed.

"Girl, don't let that stop you from getting married. You know I would be there in spirit, boo," I said, trying to make light of the situation.

"That ain't the same, and you know it! I swear, I really wish you guys could come back out into general population. I really miss yo' ass."

"Me too!" was all I could say, and then there was a knock at the door.

"I know y'all niggas ain't in here partying without me." White Girl came in the room with a bottle of Dom Pérignon and three champagne glasses.

"Hell yeah! Bring that shit on in here." Coco stood and hugged White Girl, took a glass from her, and then passed me one.

"Damn! I forgot the other thing," White Girl said, putting the bottle of Dom on the dresser before she walked out.

I stood and poured myself a glass and then one for Coco, who was looking at me like I was crazy. "What?" I asked.

"Damn, that girl's starting to look old," she whispered.

"Yeah. I guess stress, drinking, and cigarettes will do that to you." I put the Dom back on the dresser.

"Yo', her ass need a damn makeover," Coco said just as White Girl returned with a big-ass box of chocolate-covered strawberries.

"Who need a makeover?" she said, eyeing us suspiciously.

"Oh…I was just tellin' L that I wish I would've brought all of my stuff so we could do makeovers—you know, just for fun, girl," Coco said with a smile, cleaning up her mess.

"Yeah, we sure could use them!" I added to play along.

* * *

We stayed up late into the night watching movies and playing cards, just like the old days. It was six in the morning before I went to bed, but Maine ass insisted on waking me up at ten thirty. "Boo, get up." He shook me, and I pretended to still be asleep, hoping he would get the hint and leave me alone. "Lovely, I know you ain't sleepin'." He shook me again.

Annoyed, I sat up. "You right! How can I sleep with you in here bothering me?" I looked at him with my eyes half-open.

"Listen, I got something to take care of. I'm leavin', and I'll be back a little later." He sat on the edge of the bed and slipped on his white Air Force Ones.

"You woke me up to tell me that?" I yawned.

"You got a smart-ass mouth, you know that? No. I woke yo' mean ass up to tell you I got some people coming by the crib today for you and your girls. I know you don't want to go out, so I figured I would have them come here. Now get yo' fine ass up and get downstairs. Breakfast is waiting." He kissed me on the cheek and was out.

About fifteen minutes later, I finally found my way downstairs. Much to my surprise, there was laughter coming from the kitchen.

"'Bout time your ass joined the party," White Girl called out from the formal dinning room right next to the kitchen.

"I thought for sure I would beat you bitches down here." I took a seat at the head of the marble-top table. Coco was to my left, and White Girl was to my right. They were almost finished with their food, so I wasted no time and dug into mine. There were so many things to choose from that it put me in the mind of a small buffet: bacon, sausage links, pancakes, waffles, eggs, grits, and fruit, just to name a few.

"Girl, we never went to sleep," Coco confessed.

"What? What did y'all do when I went to sleep?" I asked, pouring myself some orange juice.

"Girl, you know how I does it. The minute your nonsmoking ass went to bed, we fired up a blunt and played some more cards, and then next thing I knew, Maine was telling us the food was here."

Coco dapped up White Girl, who added, "Hell yeah...just in time for the munchies," And they laughed in unison.

"Y'all ain't nothing but some weed heads." I noticed that my niece, who was always up with the birds, was not at the table. "Where is Shawnie?"

"Heather from next door came and got her this morning. Her and Briana are having a sleepover tonight." White Girl went to the kitchen and returned with a bottle of Moët and poured some in her orange juice.

Coco and I looked at her like she had lost it. "Girl, it ain't even noon yet, and you drinkin' already?" I said.

"Since when is there a certain time of day to get your drink on, especially for a grown-ass woman like myself?" She held her glass up in salute and then tipped it back.

"Bitch, ain't shit wrong with having a drink now and then, but damn, girl! You been drinking like a fish since I got here," Coco said.

"Y'all need to lighten up. Ain't shit to do around this bitch but get wasted...so cheers!" This time, she held up the bottle, tipped it back, and took a huge gulp.

"Well, I guess you got a point. At least you ain't drinking an' driving. You getting fucked up in the right place...your house! Shit, come to think of it, my ass ain't driving neither. Pour me a drink. I ain't got nowhere to be." Coco laughed and held her glass out while White Girl poured as she was told.

"It don't matter whether she drinking inside or outside the house—drinkin' and drivin' or sitting right here at this table. The point is that she drinking, and it's a little too damn much if you ask me." I was getting a little upset. Since she wasn't around all the time like I was, Coco didn't really know how bad White Girl's drinking had gotten, and she seemed to be pacifying and justifying when she shouldn't have been.

"Coco, girl, L here ain't no fun. She is so uptight and don't never want to do nothing. She got everybody on edge around here," she said, talking about me like I wasn't even there.

"Excuse me for being the responsible one. While you be getting wasted, I be taking care of your fucking daughter, you fucking drunk!" I snapped and stood up to leave the room.

Coco grabbed my hand. "Lovely, don't be like that. You know that she was just playing."

"I told you she uptight!" White Girl chimed in before she took another swig from the bottle.

"Uptight? Uptight? I guess you don't think shit is real out here for us. I can't be out here all footloose and carefree, because the minute I do, I am dead! Don't you understand that?" I yelled, walking out of the room, but then I decided I wasn't finished yet, so I turned back around, "You don't think them Feds are real? What about Frankie and the mob...or—better yet—Lucifer? You think we can just get back out there and live life normal like there ain't shit goin' on? If you do, then be my guest. Go ahead and take your fool ass out there. I ain't holding nobody hostage—and like you said, you're a grown-ass woman," I seethed, pointing toward the door. The bitch was working on my nerves, and that shit was getting real old.

"Look, L, I ain't saying that shit ain't real. I was there when you had to come up in that hospital and get me, so I know it's as real as it gets, but damn! Sometimes you got to learn how to relax. I'm sorry if I stepped on your toes, because I honestly didn't mean to, but eventually you got to take a chance out there and see what happens. I'm not saying to go back to Detroit makin' all kinds of niggas-I'm-back-come-and-get-me noise, but we could leave and go on vacation to Hawaii or some-damn-where. We could at least travel to another state, or fucking Canada or Mexico, for all I care. We all need a change of scenery to get our minds right. I'm tired of being cooped up in this damn house, and I'm sure my baby and Maine are too." She sipped again.

She had a point, and I knew it, but I was scared to death and too mad to admit it.

CHAPTER 3

After our heated bickering, we put it behind us and got on with our day. At about one in the afternoon, the intercom rang. "Yes?" I said after I hit speak.

"There is gentleman by the name of James Backwards at the gate. He says you are expecting him."

I laughed and knew it was my gay friend/personal shopper, Semaj. He was always giving people the name "James Backwards" to get a laugh, because Semaj was j-a-m-e-S spelled backwards, and most people never caught on to the joke. "Yes, please send him in," I said.

Seconds later, the doorbell rang, and there was Semaj. Knowing that he came with all types of goodies, I couldn't get the door open fast enough. "Hey, girrrl," he said, sounding like the diva he was as he walked up to the door with a pile of fancy-looking boxes in his hands.

"Hey, Mr. Backwards." I kissed him on the cheek and stepped aside for him to pass.

He headed right into the media room and then went back for more.

White Girl went to help him with the portable racks, while me and Coco popped the tops of the boxes open like champagne.

"Damn, diva. Thanks for the help," he said, smacking his

glossed lips.

"Anytime. You know it's nothing," I teased. "Hey, this is my best friend Coco. Coco, this is Semaj, my godsend in the fashion world," I said, as they exchanged pleasantries.

There was Christian Dior, Chanel, Louboutins, Giuseppes, Gucci, and Louis Vuitton, along with what seemed like millions of other names and designers. You know my ass was in Heaven! I immediately began to strip my clothes off and try stuff on, not caring one bit that Semaj was there. I didn't have anything he would possibly want anyway.

"Oh my God! This shit is bad," Coco said, holding up a pair of do-me boots that were so long I knew they'd stop right in the crease of somebody's vagina. They were right up Coco's alley; she loved outrageous stuff like that.

"Only you would get some of those leather boots when it's about to be summertime," I said as I put on a pale pink Chanel baby doll dress and grabbed a matching pale pink LV purse with peanut butter-colored straps.

"This is Michigan, in May. It ain't gonna be that hot yet," she said

I nodded in agreement because she did have a point. Michigan weather was moody. "That is super hot, girl," I told White Girl, who was trying on a Dereon exclusive.

"How much is this? I may not be able to afford it. I mean, my shop is doing some thangs, yeah, but this may be out of my league," Coco asked Semaj, who was sitting on the floor lacing up these Giuseppe sandals for me.

"Girl, you must not know. Big Daddy handled the bill, okay?" He popped his lips and gave me five.

"Who in the hell is Big Daddy?" she asked, and we all fell out laughing.

"Maine, girl. Semaj calls him that," White Girl answered, wiping the tears from her eyes from laughing so hard.

"Shit! Kim on the *Housewives* had Big Papa, and this diva

here has Big Daddy with his sexy ass," Semaj added, winking at me.

We shopped until we dropped. After Coco heard that the bill was on Big Daddy Maine, she damn near got everything me and White Girl left behind, and Semaj went home with practically nothing in his inventory. "I'm going to have to kiss that nigga Maine when he gets back," Coco joked as we sat in the media room, still admiring our things long after Semaj had left.

"You and me both," I agreed.

"Yeah, L. You got a good nigga, girl. You need to stop trippin' and give that nigga what he been asking for—either a baby or a marriage, and I say do both," White Girl added.

"Shit! Is that all his fine, rich ass wants? I woulda gave him 'bout three of them by now, girl, and dragged his ass down the aisle. What are you waiting for?" Coco asked.

I knew there was no escaping the awkward conversation, but once again I was saved by the bell—this time literally when the doorbell rang. It was my wonderful masseuse Nyla and her team from Wonderful Moments, an upscale relaxation parlor. I didn't trip that the gate didn't call, because Nyla and her staff were there on the regular, at least three times a week.

"Nyla! Come in, come in." I hugged her heavy frame and then moved aside to let her do her thing.

She went right into the formal living room and began to set up and instruct her team on how I liked things. Nyla always used the living room for massages because it was perfect for the occasion. It was huge and sort of empty, with just enough furniture inside to give it that comfy-cozy feel to really set the mood. "Here you are, darling," Nyla said as she handed me three oversized plush pink robes.

I got the point and walked away to go and retrieve my girls. Within minutes, White Girl and I had stripped down to panties.

Coco, on the other hand, went fully nude. "I want the man," she said and pointed out the man standing at the foot of one of the three beds with a bottle of oil in his hand. "That nigga look like Tyrese's fine ass, don't he?" She nudged me, but I didn't respond. For one, he didn't look like no damn Tyrese, and for another thing, I liked myself a chocolate man, but not that chocolate. My men had to be a shade or two or three lighter than that blue-black dude.

"This is Antonio." Nyla pointed to her left. "And this is Tangy." She pointed to the small Asian lady who looked to be over forty but had the body of a twelve-year-old.

"You got her. You know that, right?" I told White Girl, because the lady was too damn small to work my muscles the way they needed to be worked.

"Whatever," she said, and with that we each headed to our respective tables.

They all faced the back while we got under the warm sheets. Nyla put on the CD that sounded like a tropical storm, and I instantly relaxed; it was my favorite sound to unwind to, and something about it just comforted me.

CHAPTER 4

"Ladies, I trust you all had a good day?" Maine asked as he walked into the media room, where we must've fell asleep after our massages.

"Maine, you know you my nigga, right?" Coco sat up and sprung to her feet.

"That's wassup," he said, taking a swig from his beer.

"For real, my nigga, you hooked us up. I was asking Lovely, do you got any brothers, cousins or uncles? Shit, I ain't picky." She laughed, and I did, too, even though I knew she was dead-ass serious.

"Nope, my nigga. I'm so low, wit' no family. The streets raised me," he said and pulled a blunt from behind his ear.

"And you got that good shit! Hell yeah! Fire that shit up," Coco said so loud that it caused White Girl to wake up right on cue.

I shook my head at those weed heads and then excused myself to take a shower while they got high. I lay back in the Jacuzzi tub with a lot on my mind. It had been a really great day, and I was so thankful to have a man like Maine in my life. He had such a big heart, and not only did he go out of his way to make special moments like that happen for me, but also for my friends. That meant a lot to me. I knew that to the onlookers, I was crazy as hell not to be falling over myself trying to get him down the aisle, but

I had my reasons. Every single day, I thought about how much love I thought my father had for my mother, but then he ended up having her killed and her body stuffed inside a box to be taken out like yesterday's garbage. To make matters worse, my Maine was the killer hired for the job—not to mention the fact that he was there when my sister Tori took her last breath. I understand that he didn't know either of them were my kin, but that didn't make me feel any better about the situation. Over the years, I'd come to terms with that, and I knew that had he known they were my family, he never would've have done the things he did. But I still thought about it.

There was a knock at the door. "Hey, baby. How was your day?" Maine walked in and took a seat on the toilet.

"It was wonderful. Thank you for treating the girls and me. We had a blast." I leaned out of the soapy water and kissed his perfectly made lips.

"You know that's how I roll. It was nothing. Them yo' peeps, so they my peeps too." He leaned back with his eyes barely open, and I could tell he was good and high.

"How was your day?" I asked as I sat back on the bath pillow.

"You know—just business as usual, boo, but yo, let me holla at you right quick." He sat up.

"Damn!" was what I wanted to say, but instead I just nodded for him to continue.

"What I got to do to make you happy, L?"

"Maine, please don't start. You know I'm happy already." I closed my eyes to hide my frustration.

"You can't be!" He stood. "If you was happy, then you would want to make me happy in return." He raised his voice, which was a very bad habit of his, but I was used to it.

"So you saying you ain't happy?" I raised my tone to match his, and I was shocked as hell when he didn't respond with a *"No."* Hell, I would've even taken a *"Yes,"* but when he didn't respond at all, that hurt me the most.

* * *

I finished bathing and then went to find my girls. They were at the kitchen table playing a game of speed when I walked in.

"You good?" Coco asked and then put an end to the card game.

"Where is Maine?" I asked, wanting to make sure he wasn't in earshot of the conversation.

"He said he needed some air. He grabbed his car keys and left," White Girl added.

"Well," I sighed and continued, "look...y'all know he been pushing this marriage thing, and y'all know if it wasn't for this situation we in, then I would say 'yes' in a heartbeat but—"

"But what, Lovely?" Coco asked, cutting me off. "Damn! This nigga love your last year's panties, and your ass is about to mess that up. He is a real nigga, and he got your back 100 percent. Why can't you see that?" Coco gave a pleading look.

"I understand all that, but you of all people should know where I'm coming from with my hesitation. You was there when my father cashed Lena out and treated her the way Maine is treating me, and you also know that the nigga switched the game up on her ass in a New York minute—as soon as she changed and wasn't his idea of perfection, he put that bitch in a fucking box!" I hit the table, causing the cards to scatter.

"Maine ain't Lucifer though, Lovely. That's what you keep forgetting. Your father is four kinds of crazy, a whole different breed of nigga. You can't charge Maine with the actions of your father."

She tried to get me to smile, but I wasn't in the mood. I had a lot on my mind, and I needed to get my shit together quick fast and in a hurry, before I lost the last good thing I had to left to hold on to.

"L, you know I always tell you that there ain't too many good men left in the world, and the fact that you got one should make you hold on to him and never want to let go. Ya' feel me? My good man didn't make it down the altar or to see our daughter grow up, and that kills me more and more every day. I'm telling you, woman to woman and friend to friend, that you need to come down off whatever it is that you're trippin' on and save your relationship."

I had to admit to myself that they were both right, but the whole thing had me buggin'. "I just wish this thing was different. It's not just marriage or babies that's got me vexed. It's the fear that this shit ain't over, and even though I'm tired of hiding I ain't ready for war again." I rubbed my temples. "For real, I'm just sick of this lifestyle. You feel me?"

"I can most definitely understand that shit. That's why I just say 'fuck it' and come out wit' cha pistols poppin'." Coco laughed as she pulled a blunt from behind her ear and lit it up.

I watched as she puffed twice, releasing the smoke from her nostrils, and then I listened as she began to choke. "I wish I could, but it's more than just me involved in this shit. Everybody saying it's been long enough, but my gut is telling me some shit is going to pop off the minute I let my guard down. I got too many enemies to be acting like everything is gravy, and I'm just trippin'." I laid my head down on the table.

"Well, Ms. Brown, the fact that the nigga is riding with you when he don't have to, speaks volumes to me. This ain't his beef, and it ain't his battle, but he by your side, so if the nigga want to be married, then I say you should marry that man! If some shit go down, at least you know he is going to have your back just like he did the last time," Coco added and then passed the blunt to White Girl.

"You know what? When you're right you're right! I'm sick of playing possum." I popped my head up from the table. I was tired of hiding and waiting for something to happen. The fact was, if anything was really gonna go down, it would happen regardless of how well I hid. It was Michigan, home of Detroit, and if a nigga really wanted beef, they wouldn't wait for you to come out. They would bring it right up to your front door! "Now, let me go and find my man to let him know we can do this thing tomorrow if he still wants to!"

"'Bout damn time!" they said in unison and cracked up.

CHAPTER 5

After I gave him the good news, we made love all night long. He couldn't believe I was serious, and to tell the truth, neither could I.

"Good morning, baby," Maine said, rolling on top of our red silk sheets and exposing his sexy, brown, chiseled body.

I kissed him on his impeccably shaped mouth. "Good morning."

"So when do you want to get married?" He eyed me suspiciously, and I smiled.

"I was thinking that today would be perfect, because I've made you wait long enough. Besides, there's no time like the present, right?" I squealed with excitement.

Now he was the one smiling, exposing his perfectly aligned, cocaine-white teeth. "You for real?" he quizzed.

I stood from the bed and headed to our huge walk-in closet to search for something to wear. I'd picked up a little weight over the years from spending so much of my time indoors, but my twenty-five-year-old body carried my Size Seven well. "Yes, I'm serious. Are you?"

"Damn right. I can have someone over here in twenty minutes—that's just how serious I am!" he yelled from our private bathroom on the other side of the room.

I pulled out a knitted brown and beige Versace top, a pair of tan slacks, some brown Guiseppe shoe boots, and my jewelry. "No need to have someone come over. Let's just go to the courthouse."

He stepped from the bathroom and looked at me like I was crazy. "What?" was all he said.

"Last night, after talking to Coco, I came to the conclusion that I'm sick of living in fear. She told me to say 'fuck it' and pop pistols if I have to." I laughed.

"Oh yeah. No doubt about that! We got heat for niggas that want beef, but are you sure you're ready though?"

"As long as I have you by my side, I'm as ready as I'll ever be. I just want to make sure you fully understand what could happen once we resurface again," I said, walking over to him.

"Yeah baby I know, but trust me when I tell you that I ain't gon' let none of them fools touch you. Please believe they gon' hafta get through me first," he said, pointing at himself.

I grabbed his hand and looked him in the eyes. "Baby, I know you got me when it comes to the streets, but the alphabet boys is something totally different. You know they want LB for those drug charges—not to mention the shootout at the hospital—so I just want you to be clear about what it is that you're getting into."

"Don't worry, ma'! I got you! Now, let's go get married before you change your damn mind."

CHAPTER 6

In thirty minutes, we had dressed and were headed downstairs to the smell of bacon.

"Why y'all so dressed up?" White Girl asked as she slid a piece of toast onto Shawnie's plate.

"Well, girl, I know you will be glad to know we are going to get married today," I announced, flashing a huge smile.

"Now, before I up and get all excited about this, tell me you're serious," she said, standing there in her black pajamas, with her hair wrapped up and some kind of greenish cream all over her face, cheesing from ear to ear.

"Yes, I'm so for real. We are going to the Justice of the Peace, and we want you and Coco to come and be our witnesses," I said, kissing my niece on the forehead while she sat at the kitchen counter, swinging her legs back and forth.

"Of course! I would love to be your witness. Can you put Shawnie on the bus for me while I go upstairs and get dressed?" she asked as she took her scarf off and unwrapped her hair. Coco had dyed it platinum blonde, giving her a true Caucasian look.

"Yeah, girl. Go 'head," I said, pulling out my cell phone to call Coco, who had to leave around three in the morning when she got a call from Zo, telling her that one of her boys was sick.

"Hey, Leslie. Wassup?" she asked, using my code name in

case the phone was tapped.

"Girl, we're doing it today. Meet me at the court building in downtown Detroit at noon," I said and then listened to her scream for about four minutes straight. I glanced up at the clock and noticed that it was eight forty-five, so I helped Shawnie down from the kitchen stool, grabbed her book bag, and we made our way to the bus stop. "You finished yet?" I asked Coco as I zipped up Shawnie's jacket when we got outside.

"Girl, I don't know what I'm more excited about—your wedding or having you back in the city again, bitch."

We laughed as my niece and I made the ten-foot journey to the bus stop, where we waited and watched as the bus turned down our street.

"Girl, I can't wait to be back in the city either. It's like a breath of fresh air Coco, I swear. I'm so glad you talked me into it." The bus pulled right up as it always, and I bent down to give Shawnie a tight hug. "I love you, little girl, and don't you ever forget that, okay? Now, have a good day at school. Learn something good, and I will see you later, all right?" I kissed her on her forehead.

"Okay, Auntie L. See you when I come home. Can we play dolls today?" she asked, reaching up to hug me back. "You promised," she reminded me as she stepped on the school bus. I nodded and watched her walk down the aisle, and then I waved at her through the window as she took her seat.

"What are you wearing?" Coco chimed in, catching my attention as I watched the bus pull off.

My gaze fell upon a man parked across the street from my house. He was looking directly at me. My eyes widened not because I was scared, but because there was something in his eyes that put me on alert. He had a menacing scowl on his face, and I couldn't shake the bad feeling that I was getting from the stranger. I had never seen him—not once—during the many days when I window-watched my cul-de-sac before. "What the fuck?" I spoke out loud as the man pulled off.

"Huh, Leslie?" I heard from the phone.

I didn't respond. I just hung up and ran into the house, almost knocking Maine down as he was opening the door to come outside.

"Damn, baby! What's the matter?"

"It was him! I saw him. Out there!" I pointed at the car as it scurried off of my block.

"Who?" White Girl asked as she came out of the house, turning to lock the door.

"I really don't know who, but the man I just saw across the street looked like he was up to something bad, and when we made eye contact he pulled away," I said, still looking down the block.

"Baby, don't punk out on me now. He was probably lost or just visiting someone, that's all," he tried to reassure me as we walked over to his brand new 2011 silver and blue Maybach 62.

"It was just your mind playing tricks on you. Girl, you can't be getting cold feet already! You just decided to get married hours ago," White Girl added, and we all laughed.

CHAPTER 7

On the way back to Detroit, I couldn't stop thinking about the stranger and what his deal was, but the closer that we got to the city, I decided to let it go. My thoughts drifted over to my brother. Even though we weren't blood, nobody could tell. He always had my back. Do It was my right-hand man and my security, but most importantly, he was my friend. I knew he would've been so happy for me on my wedding day, and that was when the guilt started to kick in. It really fucked with me that he ended up dead just because he knew me. If it weren't for me, he would have been there with his family. Instead, he was just ashes in a vase, and that was my fault. I say "somewhere" because after we left Detroit, we had to cut ties with everybody. A few months later, I called Coco, and she informed me that someone in the 'hood gave him a wonderful home-going. She said everything was red and black, his favorite colors, but the casket was closed because he was unrecognizable. After the funeral, she was told he was cremated, but she didn't know who kept his urn because his mother had died years earlier, and he had no other family that anyone knew of. As I thought about it during our ride to the JP, a light came on in my head, and I made a mental note to check with the funeral director to see where my brother's urn was. It was time to bring my nigga home, where he belonged.

"We're here, baby. You ready?" Maine asked as we exited the luxury vehicle.

"Let's do this," I replied, opening my door and stepping out with Maine's assistance. I scanned the area, and for the most part, it looked normal and boring. There were a few people waiting at the bus stop, some business people in suits carrying briefcases, rushing to and from the buildings downtown, police cars patrolling the area, and meter maids coming around to give out those beloved parking tickets. Nothing looked out of place at first, but as we walked up the stairs, I began feeling sick for some reason. Nervousness hit me right in the pit of my stomach. The funny thing about it was, I wasn't nervous that I was out in the open and at any moment, I could be spotted by the many men that wished death on me; instead, I was nervous because in a matter of minutes, I'd be someone's wife.

I wondered what was supposed to happen after we both said, *"I do."* Life, for us, would never be normal, and to be honest, I still had some reservations lurking in the back of my mind about my future husband. I can't stress enough that I knew Maine loved me, but he was still a contract killer, after all. *What if my enemy calls him and puts the right price on my head? Will he take the job?* I knew he would never do it just for the money, because he had plenty of that on his own, but I didn't know if he would do it just for the sport of it. Most killers don't kill because they have to; they kill because it's a high for them, like no other drug on the planet. They enjoy the hunt, the chase, and the excitement of watching and waiting for the right moment to take down their prey, and they will pull out all the stops to get the job done. That shit alone made me uneasy, because the more I thought about it, the past five years could've been part of some big plan all along. The thought of that really had my mind racing. *How did he know I was on the bus that night when he saved me from Lucifer and that bus-driving goon? What if he's still communicating and working with Lucifer when he leaves for jobs, and what if Lucifer has known where I've been this whole time? What if this marriage bullshit is just some plot to get me out in the open?* "Fuck!" I said under my breath just as we walked up to the counter.

The clerk, a heavy woman with thick glasses, a terrible haircut, and a god-awful paisley dress smiled at us. "Are you here to get married?"

"Yes we are." Maine beamed.

I just rolled my eyes. I couldn't believe I had let myself fall for it. If I'd learned anything in life, it was that if something seems to good to be true, it probably is. I had to find a way out of there, and quick. "Where is the bathroom?" I asked with a faint smile on my face.

"Right down the hall to the left. Got the jitters, huh?" She grinned a big buck-tooth smile at me.

"No. I just need to use it," I answered, but what I really wanted to say was, *"Hell fuck yeah I'm scared bitch and if you knew better, yo' ass should be scared too! This nigga probably already made the call for them to come shoot up the court building like some old gangster-type shit before we left the house this morning.* I turned to Maine. "Give me five minutes, okay?"

He nodded, not fazed at all.

I booked down the hall, not noticing that White Girl was hot on my trail. "L, what up? You acting kinda funny and shit. What's the matter?" she asked as we entered the dingy, stale, yellow restroom that smelled like sour mop water.

"Look my nigga, it was a mistake to come here. We need to get the fuck out of Dodge," I said, pacing back and forth like some damn caged lion at the zoo, contemplating my next move.

I heard someone flush, and Coco emerged from the stall. "What do you mean it was a mistake?" she asked. "What the hell happened between eight forty-five and now?" she asked as she washed her hands.

I was so mad that I couldn't even find the words to express to them what I was feeling.

"Girl, what is it?" White Girl asked.

"Yeah, Lovely. What's wrong with you? Are you just nervous? If you are, don't be, because…"

She kept talking, but I didn't hear any of it because my heart was beating so loud that it was the only sound I was able to hear. Even though Coco was just at my house and I was thanking her for all that good advice she gave me, I kind of wanted to slap the shit out of her for letting me fall for the stupid shit, but I brushed it off because she really had no clue as to what was going on. She and White Girl hugged me tight, even though I'm sure they didn't know why. As I stood in the embrace, I was able to take a deep breath and calm down, allowing my heart rate to return to normal. Finally, my mouth started to work again. "Girl, I just feel like something ain't right. When we were walking up the stairs to come in, I began to think about how Maine is a contract killer, and him putting us up in his house could've been the plan all along so that Lucifer will know exactly where I'm at all the damn time. Then I thought about how he was pushing this marriage issue, and now we're here out in the open, with no weapons. They could be coming to shoot this bitch up at any moment y'all," I said with urgency.

They both looked at me like I was crazy. "First of all L," White Girl said, "Maine wanted to have someone come to the house to marry y'all. You were the one who mentioned the courthouse, and you also picked today. Remember? You told me that earlier."

Coco added, with a little frustration in her voice, "Lovely, I'm a little tired of hearing this. If he wanted to get you, you'd be got by now. You've been in that place for over five years. He could've killed you a million times—in your sleep, in the shower, or while you were cooking and had your back turned. If Maine wanted you dead, he would not have been willing to bring you out in a courthouse with all these witnesses around. He would've done that shit at your house because nobody knows you live there, and the 'hood thinks you're far, far away. Nobody, besides my ass would come looking for you."

As I took in what she said, I came to the conclusion that once again, she was right, and I felt like a dumb ass. I had no other choice but to brush off my negative vibes. "You're absolutely right girl. Now let me go get my man before he changes his mind. He's already been waiting about twenty minutes, and I know y'all hoes are sick of me." We shared a laugh, and I brushed my hair, fixed my make-up, took a deep breath, and proceeded to the door.

Just as I reached for the handle, the door burst open, slamming hard against the wall and causing all of us to jump back in shock. It was Maine, looking like a wild man, and I knew something wasn't right. "Come on! We gotta go NOW!" he yelled.

"Why? What happened?" I said as fear gripped my heart.

"Yo, Shawnie's school called my cell. They said she never showed up for kindergarten this morning." He looked at me with panic all over his face.

"What?!" White Girl screamed, instantly turning paler than she normally was.

"Bullshit! I put her on that bus myself this morning!" I said in disbelief.

"I know, Ma. That's why we gotta get over there and see what the fuck is going on." He turned toward the door, and we all ran out of the court building in a panic.

I didn't know what was going on, so I told Coco to go home and that I would call her later. I silently prayed it was just some big misunderstanding, like maybe she fell asleep on the bus and they took her back to the bus terminal or something like that. I had seen that on the news a time or two. *Yeah, that's gotta be it,* I told myself, but I didn't believe it deep down.

CHAPTER 8

On the ride home, White Girl stayed on the phone with the school while they searched high and low for my niece. Maine did almost ninety miles per hour all the way. Once we were back in Ann Arbor, we headed straight to the school.

There was a middle-aged woman standing at the front door to greet us. "Hello, Candace. As you know, I'm Mrs. Hilary, the principal here at Fair Lady Elementary. I want to let you know we are doing all we possibly can to locate DeShawna, and—"

White Girl was all up in her face before she could finish with her lame-ass excuses. "First of fucking all, how in the fuck do you *lose* a child? Second of all, the bus came to get her at eight forty-five, and school starts at nine. You slack-ass fuckers didn't call until twelve fifteen, It took you that long to discover that my five-year-old daughter is missing?" she grilled the lady.

"Well we don't take roll until lunchtime, to give the late students a chance to arrive," she nervously answered and held her hand out, signaling us to follow her inside the school.

"Listen lady…you need to speak with the bus driver who picked up my child this morning right in front of my goddamn door, because we know she got on that bitch this morning."

I stepped up and put my arm around her shoulders to calm her down, because I knew she was minutes from slapping the woman senseless.

"Yes, we have contacted the school Transportation Department, and they said there was a sub driver today for that bus. Unfortunately, we've uh, had some trouble tracking him down. He can't be found anywhere," Mrs. Hilary said with a pained expression on her full but wrinkled face.

"Oh my God! I can't believe this shit. Did you even think to call the police?" I chimed in. From what she was telling us, my little five-year-old niece could be anywhere in the world with some man posing as a substitute bus driver, just to be next to little children, for reasons I didn't even want to think of.

"Yes, of course. They should be here shortly," she said, looking as if she was about to have a nervous breakdown as she took a seat behind her desk.

"Well, did all the other kids get to school safely this morning on DeShawna's bus?" Maine questioned.

"Yes. Everyone was accounted for but her," Mrs. Hilary answered.

"Did you speak with the other children to see if they noticed anything?" I wondered.

"Unfortunately, kindergartners are of little help in situations like this because all of their stories are different. They don't really pay much attention to what goes on outside their own little area." She removed her glasses and placed them on her desk. "I'm afraid the eyewitnesses aren't very good when their little eyes can hardly even see over the seats."

* * *

About fifteen extremely long minutes later, two police officers knocked on the door and with Mrs. Hilary's permission, walked into the office, past me and Maine, who were sitting down on the brown faux leather couch. They walked right up to the desk where White Girl was sitting.

When they began to take information from her, I used the

opportunity to walk out. I couldn't take the risk of being recognized by the boys in blue, so I would have to do my part of this little search-and-rescue operation far from there. I went outside and hailed a cab.

Maine came out behind me and asked me where I was going.

"I can't be in there with the cops, baby. I'm going home to change my clothes, and then I'm hitting the pavement to see where my Shawnie is. You stay here. White Girl needs you…and don't forget to tell them about the weird man across the street staring at us this morning," I said through the window as the cab pulled off.

I paid the cab driver twenty bucks, even though the bill was under nine; like I said, the school was just a few blocks away from where we lived. I then grabbed my purse and walked up to my door.

To my surprise, I found a box on my doorstep addressed to me. I scooped it up and made my way inside, dropping my shoes on the mat. I ran up the stairs with the box clutched under my arm and set it on the bed, along with my purse, as I pulled a pair of denim Seven jeans and a pink and white Ed Hardy top off of the hanger in my closet. I reached under my mattress to retrieve the butcher knife I kept hidden on my side and sliced the box open to reveal a mostly empty space, all except for one white envelope. It said "READ ASAP" on the outside. Since I was in a hurry and worried about Shawnie, I quickly ripped it open right away and began to read: *"Paradise, long time no hear from…"* I lost my breath. Frankie, my mafia connect, was the only person to call me by that name. I blinked a few times and then continued reading: *"Five years is a long time honey, and I want you to know that I haven't forgot anything! In my line of business, it's always an eye for an eye, a tooth for a tooth—but in this case, it's a niece for a nephew! Call the number listed below if you want your precious nigger niece back."*

"What the fuck!" I screamed to myself. I was somewhat relieved that at least I had a clue where my niece was—and that as far as I could tell she was still alive—but I was pissed the fuck off that we had been caught slipping, and my little niece was suffering for it. I heard my front door open and close, and I picked up the knife ready for war.

"Baby, you up there?" Maine called out.

"Yeah," I replied, relieved that it was him.

Maine flew up the stairs, taking them three at a time with those strong legs of his. "I know who the fuck has our niece!" he yelled as he came through the bedroom door.

"What? How?" was all I could say before White Girl flew through the bedroom door as well.

"Lovely, Frankie has my baby!" She began to cry uncontrollably.

I looked over to Maine, who handed me a letter just like the one I had just read. I reviewed the contents, and it was the exact same letter. "Where did this come from?" I asked him.

"It was in the driver seat when we got ready to leave the school," Maine answered, beads of sweat forming on his forehead.

"I got a copy of it off the front porch," I said, holding mine up.

Maine took it, looked it over then tossed it on the bed. "This muthafucka got some balls. When I see him, he's a dead man. I swear on my life." He went to the closest, opened the floor safe, and started grabbing guns that I didn't even know were in there.

I looked up at a still-sobbing White Girl and a mad-as-hell Maine. I couldn't find the words to speak. Part of me was still really confused because I didn't know what the hell was going on. *How in the hell did they find us, and why did they wait all this time to retaliate?*

"If these fucking Italians want a war, then call his ass and tell him to bring it on," Maine said, snapping me out of my daze.

I went over to the bed and reached inside my purse to retrieve my cell phone. I pressed the number from the note into my phone and held my breath for what seemed like an hour.

"Paradise, is that you?" a man answered, using the name I gave Frankie when we first met and I was a call girl with After Hours. At first, "Paradise" was the stage name I used when I danced at Rump Shaker Gentleman's Club with Coco, but when that club was burned down, I ended up working for a guy named Black, who owned a call girl service. Frankie was my first client, and shortly after that, he became my business partner. When I made the decision to become a drug dealer to sabotage the game and avenge my sister's death, it was Frankie who put me on with the best products at a dirt-cheap rate, believing me to be the middleman—or middle woman—between him and my boss LB, who was of course really me. After Frankie's nephew Anthony was killed and a million dollars was stolen by this alleged LB, Frankie put a bounty on my head because he didn't know who LB was, and he felt that I was responsible because I vouched for LB.

"Where is Frankie and where the fuck is my niece?" I cut to the chase because I knew it wasn't Frankie on the phone.

"Frankie is busy and let's just say your niece is safe...for now," he said with a wicked laugh.

"Enough of this bullshit. Tell me what the fuck I gotta do to get her back." I sat on the edge of the bed and gripped the comforter.

"Okay. I see you're not in a joking mood, so I'll get right to it. I was told by a little birdie that your boss still has Frankie's muthafuckin' money. He wants it back—every dime, plus a million for each year we've had to wait on it. Call it interest. That's six million in all. He also wants this LB nigger served up on a platter. You come up with the money then LB and you can have your precious nigger niece. She's not my type, but a few of my soldiers would love to see what that five-year-old pussy feels like," he threatened.

I almost threw up right then and there. I couldn't believe his nasty ass was talking about having someone rape my little kindergarten niece. "Don't you fuckin' touch her! So you hear me, you fuckin' bastard? Don't nobody lay one fuckin' nasty-ass finger on that girl!" I screamed.

White Girl began to go crazy at the mention of someone touching her baby.

"You've got until next Friday to get this done. I'll be in touch to let you know when and where all of this goes down." *Click.*

"Well? What did he say?" Maine and White Girl asked simultaneously.

"He said he wants six million dollars and LB by next Friday or…or…" I clenched my jaw.

"Or what?" Maine asked in a bit of an irritated yell.

I looked up at as the tear slipped down my cheek. "Or he's gonna let his men have their way with Shawnie."

"Oh my God! Not my…my baby! Lovely, what am I going to do? I can't let this happen! Oh my God!" White Girl cried hysterically.

I could do nothing to console her because I was in a bad mental space myself. The shit was starting to give me a headache, and I just wished I would've ended all of it five years earlier by leaving the game before it tore us apart.

"Fuck it! If he want LB, then we will give him LB," Maine said as he headed for the bedroom door.

"Huh? What do you mean? How can we do that?" White Girl asked.

"I'm going to the bank to get the money—or at least what I can of it. When I come back, you're gon' call that muthafucka back and tell him you have LB. I will turn myself in," he said.

I stood, shaking my head furiously. I couldn't let it go down like that. "No, Maine. I'm not letting you take the fall for me. This is my mess, and I'm going to fix it. You don't have to pretend to be LB, but I do need you to get that money for me if you can," I said and began to pace the floor thinking of a master plan. Although I didn't really know what was going on nor what to expect, I prepared myself for the worst. If the Italians wanted a bloodbath, that was exactly what I would bring to the table. *Fuck Lucifer and fuck Frankie, because I ain't losing no more family to the streets!* The shit was about to go down one way or another, and I hoped I'd still be standing when the smoke cleared.

CHAPTER 9

Maine

Man, what the fuck is going on? I thought to myself as I hopped in my car and sped to the bank. I had several accounts all over the globe, but this one was the closest. Even though I knew it didn't hold all the money I needed, I was prepared to go to bank after bank and beat the streets until I came up with all of it before the sun went down. Six million wasn't shit to me; I'd been stacking bread for as long as I could remember. When I first got in the game, I watched the OGs, as well as the young niggas my age, and I came to the conclusion that the OGs definitely did things better. I followed their lead, and life was good. I could blow stacks all day every day if I wanted to, but I was way too low-key for that. I was a simple man, and I liked my lifestyle to be simple. Having money is nice, but I hate the type of people money attracts, like gold diggers and fake-ass friends.

My father was never around, and for the most part, neither was my mama. She picked me up from school one day and dropped me off over at my Great Aunt Sophia's house. She told me she loved me and said she had to go.

"Why mama?" my twelve-year-old self asked my young twenty-five-year-old mother.

"For reasons you will never understand son." Was all she said, as she quickly wiped a tear away.

"Mama, please don't leave me here," I begged as she looked away from me.

"Jermaine son, I gotta go. You be a good boy. Grow up and make ya' mama proud." She smiled at me, fighting back tears.

"When you coming back?" I stared at her and she frowned.

"I'm not son. Now no more questions okay. Get your bag out of the trunk and go tell Aunt Sophia you're here."

"But, Mama—"

"Jermaine, go on now. I love you son. You remember that, all right?" she said.

I got my bag and watched my mother leave.

The entire first year at my aunt's house, I expected my mother to return, so I never got too comfortable in my room. I kept all my things in my suitcase so I would be ready for her when she came back to get me, but she never did. Time and time again, I asked my aunt why my mother left me, and her only response was, "because she had to." It really puzzled me, because my mother was a good person who hung out with good people. She never did drugs or even took a drink in her life. Although she was young when she had me, she did her best to care for me. She went to work every day so we could afford to stay in a nice, middle-class neighborhood and have nice things. It was just me and Mom—no boyfriends or anything like that—so I wondered how and why she could just up and leave me when I was all she had.

It wasn't until I turned fourteen, and my sixty-four-year-old aunt was dying of breast cancer, that she finally told me my mother was a cold-blooded killer who got paid for what she did. "After years of crime, the cops finally caught up with her for a murder she committed in New York, and she had to make a choice between turning herself in or taking you on the run with her," she said weakly. I was too shocked to say anything; I just looked at my dying aunt with my mouth wide open. "She was a good mother,

Jermaine, so she dropped you off to me and turned herself in." She coughed, and I handed her a cup of water from her bedside table.

"So how long she gotta be in jail?" I asked.

"Jermaine, baby, your mother was sentenced to death row because at the time when she was found guilty, they had the death penalty there in New York." She sipped from the glass and then reached for my hand as I cried for the first time since my mother had driven off two years prior.

* * *

Aunt Sophia passed away in her sleep two weeks after our conversation, and I feared that if I told someone about her death, they would put me in foster care, so I stayed in that house for days with her dead body. I still went to school every day because I knew that if I didn't, the school would send the truancy officers out to my house to check up on me. I ate leftovers until they were gone, and then I moved on to cereal and milk. Going into the second week, I could no longer take the smell of her decaying body, so I did what I had seen in the movies: I got sheets, blankets, and duct tape and wrapped her slim frame inside. I used a wooden clothespin to hold my nostrils closed because it smelled so bad. I put on Aunt Sophia's apron and a pair of her blue rubber gloves that she used to wash the dishes and clean the bathtub, and then I dragged her body to the back door. I had no clue where to put her, so I stood there and thought for a minute. When I heard the doorbell, I sneaked up to the peephole and saw Jimmy, a young dude from around the way who used to come by to see if my aunt needed him to do anything for her. He was rolling dope in the streets, but he always looked out for the elders on the block and slipped them money for groceries or bills from time to time. "Aunt Sophia ain't home, Jimmy," I told him.

"What's up shortstop?" he asked, looking me up and down.

"Nothing man. Bout' to do my homework. My aunt ain't here though." I looked behind me and then back at him.

"Yo, what the fuck you got going on in there, lil nigga? Why yo' ass acting all suspicious?" He looked at me, waiting on my response.

Since I didn't know what to say, I tried to close the door, but he was much older and stronger than me and managed to push his way inside. "Jimmy, man, you gotta go," I said.

He immediately held his nose. "Goddamn! What the fuck done died up in here?" He walked into the kitchen and stared at the large mass on the floor, then looked at me with curiosity. "Tell me this ain't what I think it is."

"It is," I confirmed. "She died in her sleep last week and I ain't want nobody to know cuz I don't want to go to foster care," I said, relived to get the burden off of my chest, even if it meant trouble for me.

"Damn, lil man," he said. He took a seat at the wooden kitchen table and scratched his chin like he was thinking about something important. After about five minutes, he began to talk again. "Look shortstop, I can understand why you did what you did, and because you got heart, I'ma help you out." And that was exactly what he did.

We loaded her into the back of a van, and he drove her body off into the night, promising that he'd "handle" the rest.

To my surprise, a few days later, Jimmy showed back up with a proposition for me. "Hey shortstop, I commend you on how you handled your business with the dead body and all. Most kids your age would not have lasted a few hours in your situation, let alone two weeks."

"I did what I had to do," I replied.

"No doubt, I feel that 100. I know them bills gon' start rolling in soon, and if that shit don't get paid, they will come knocking. I know you don't want that, right?" he asked.

I nodded.

"Well, I know some people who's hiring, and I think you are a good candidate for the position." He pulled out a joint and lit it.

"What type of job is it, and how much does it pay?" I asked.

"To be frank with you shortstop, you would be the person called when my mans an' dem got a beef. You would come in and make everything right, if you know what I'm saying." He made a trigger motion with his fingers.

"A…a killer?" I whispered.

He nodded.

It was at that moment of desperation that I decided if a life of murder was good enough for my mother, it would be good enough for me too.

* * *

As the time passed, I excelled at what I did. I guess it runs in the family, because I took my craft seriously. Pretty soon, I had more business than I knew what to do with. I paid my aunt's house off and made sure the bills stayed paid on the regular. I stacked dollar after dollar and became a millionaire when I was about sixteen, but even back then, I wasn't flashy.

Whenever I did hit the clubs, I always felt that the niggas throwing money in there and causing a scene with their flashy chains and flamboyant attitudes really never had shit in their pockets. If a nigga's getting dough for real, the last thing they would do would be advertise it for all the world to see. When all the other knuckleheads my age were dropping out of school because they thought the little money they were making would set them up for life, I made sure I went to school every day. I knew something those fools forgot: Knowledge is power, and I used my time in computer class to study and improve the art of my craft by researching laws that could be used against me if I was ever caught. I also researched ways to avoid getting caught. I graduated with honors and had a few scholarship offers, but I declined. People go to college in hopes of finding a good-paying job and getting rich, but I was already that, so I passed. Instead, I went out and purchased exotic cars and real estate all over the world, knowing that if I ever came across hard times, those would be of real value. As long as I owned them, I would never be broke.

BEEEEEEEP!

The horn from someone's car behind me snapped me out of my blast from the past, and I realized I had caused all the cars in my lane to miss the green light while I was deep in thought.

CHAPTER 10

I pulled up to the bank, whipped into the parking lot, cut the ignition off, and made my way to the door. My mind raced as I contemplated what the fuck was happening. Just that morning, I was about to marry the woman of my dreams, but now my niece was somewhere with a sick-ass stranger, probably scared for her life. Even though I had the money, I felt like I should be doing more, but my hands were tied. I couldn't call any of my old connects from my days in the streets because nearly all of them worked for my old boss, Lovely's dad Lucifer.

"Yes, can I help you, sir?" a Caucasian teller asked as I walked up to the counter and leaned down.

"I need to speak with Brian Heard, please," I said, asking for my connect at the bank. Brian kept my money concealed in some dummy account associated with a fake bank loan he had given me for a supposed business. He said the IRS watched accounts periodically, and any amounts over $10,000 would raise a red flag, so he created several accounts under fake names with my money. Every time I needed huge amounts of dough, Brian worked shit out, simple as that.

"Um, I think he is at lunch, but I can help you if you like." She was flirting with me, and I tried to hide my irritation.

"Look baby girl…um…Bridgette," I said, peeping her nametag,

"I need Brian like ASAP, so please tell him J. Williams is here." I didn't state my whole name because I didn't think it was necessary—or safe.

She glanced behind her and then held up her finger, signaling me to wait a moment. She walked back toward an office, and I tried not to laugh as baby girl swayed her pancake ass back and forth as hard as she could. A few seconds later, she returned to the counter and said Brian was ready for me.

I walked into the small burgundy office in the rear of the building. I didn't get a good vibe from Brian, as I sensed his hesitation and noticed the nervous look on his face. "Mr. Williams," he said, "please take a seat."

"Yo, my dude. What the fuck is the matter? I ain't even told you why I'm here yet," I said, still standing.

He pushed his glasses up on his pale face and nervously tapped on the computer screen. "Well, Mr. Williams, I don't know how to tell you this, but—"

"But what?" I snapped, impatiently interrupting him. He was beginning to really piss me off, and there was no time for it because I had shit to do.

"Apparently, the accounts I had your money in were frozen about an hour ago."

When he stood, I stepped up, ready to knock his pasty white geek ass back down. My jaws clenched, and my muscle tensed up. "*All* of them?"

"Yes." He began to sweat grenades.

"How in the fuck did you manage to fuck this up, huh? I thought you said you know what the hell you're doing? Shit! You took the money I paid you like you knew what you were doing." I slammed my fists on his desk, causing his name plate to fall off.

"I didn't fuck it up, Mr. Williams! It was frozen by the…the FBI!" he spat.

The mention of the Feds caused my heart to skip a beat. "What?" I asked for clarification before I finally took a seat in one of the black leather chairs facing his desk. My knees were too weak to stand on.

"I don't have any further information—just that your the account have been frozen, and there is a note stating that if you are spotted by anyone, they are to stall you and call somebody named Agent Nichols. See?" He turned the screen toward me, and sure as shit, that was exactly what the computer said.

"Fuck!" I shouted.

"Look, you need to leave now. If they were able to trace you through these dummy accounts I set up for you with a bogus Social, name, date of birth, and everything else, they're probably watching your every move. I don't know what you did, but you need to get out of here fast."

He was right. I needed to move and move quick. Just as I gathered my thoughts, there came a knock at the door. We both froze.

"Mr. Heard, there are some people out here to see you. It appears to be urgent," said a shaky female voice from the other side of the door.

"Veronica, tell them I'll be with them shortly," he answered.

I had begun to sweat grenades myself. When he pointed over to the window, I got the hint. I opened the window and stepped out.

Just as I made my way around the back of the building, I saw a few agents surrounding my ride. "Damn," I said and turned in the other direction, trying not to be noticed, but it was too late.

"Stop! We have a few questions," I heard one of them say as I began to run as fast as I could.

I scanned the parking lot to see what would be the quickest way out. As my luck would have it, a teenage delivery boy was getting out of his car, and he left it running. He grabbed his pizza bag and ran into the back door of the pizza place that was in the plaza with the bank, and I hopped right into the driver seat and sped off. Fifty Cent blared through the speakers as I tried to evade the two cars that had caught on and were in pursuit of me. I grabbed my phone and called my baby, Lovely.

"Hey baby. Did you get it?" she asked in a hopeful voice.

"Look boo…when I got to the bank, my accounts were closed, and—"

"What?!" she said, cutting me off.

"Yeah, but listen…the Feds were there looking for me, and now they are chasing—"

"Maine I'm so sorry I got you into this," she interrupted again.

"Listen girl!" I yelled. "Get out of that house. I'm not sure if they know about it yet, but I ain't one to take chances." I hit a hard left on Franklin, trying to lose them, but my plan only got rid of one of them; the other one was right behind me.

"Maine bring them here. I'm who they're looking for," she snapped.

"Girl are you crazy? Why would I do that?" I asked just as I hit a dip that sent the small Escort up and then down really hard, causing the CDs the youngster had tucked into his visor flying to the floor. My head hit the top of the small car and my knees hit the dashboard, but I was on a mission, so I never dropped my cell phone or lost control of the car.

"Please just trust me and do what I asked you to do."

She begged and begged until I reluctantly agreed. Minutes later, I pulled up in front of the house, just as she and White Girl stepped outside. Some lady agent ran up to my window with her gun pointed at me, yelling at the top of her lungs.

CHAPTER 11

Lovely

"Get out of the fuckin' car now, jackass!" I heard as some chick ran up to a pizza delivery car that had just stopped in front of my house.

Maine got out with his hands up and she was about to cuff him, but I called out, "He ain't who you looking for!"

She looked up at me, cuffed him anyway, and then walked him up to where me and White Girl was standing. "And you are?" she asked with attitude.

"You're looking for LB, right?" I folded my arms.

She looked confused. "What kind of game are you playing? This is LB." She tugged at Maine's handcuffs.

"You got it twisted," I began, but the sound of a speeding car coming to a screeching halt stole my attention.

"Lane you all right?" Another agent asked as she emerged from the car with two men.

"Yeah Nichols, I'm good—just got myself the notorious LB. Not bad for a rookie with two weeks under my belt, huh?" She smiled like she actually knew what she was talking about.

Nichols frowned. "Rookie, don't get too excited. That is not LB." She pointed at Maine and then continued. "Read your case files next time. That is Jermaine Williams, and she is Lovely

Brown," she said, pointing at me.

"But I thought you said we were at the bank to get LB," Lane began to whine.

Getting annoyed, Nichols patted Lane on her back and told her to wait in the car. We all looked on as she did what she was told, but she was obviously unhappy about it.

"Listen, I'm very tired today and I don't feel like playing any games, so to be real, let's just get straight to it. Where is this LB?" The seasoned vet looked to be in her late forties or early fifties.

None of us bothered to answer.

"Goddammit! If somebody don't start talking, then both of you, Jermaine and Lovely, will be going down for it all. That includes the dope we found at those stash houses in Detroit and the murder of Tori Brown, not to mention the hospital shootout. We know that was you because we have the tapes to prove it," she snarled, pointing a manicured finger at me.

"How are you going to charge me for my sister's murder?" I asked, finally breaking my silence.

"Oh, so now you got something to say? Well that's easy! Either you start talking and give me what I want, or you are both going down." She folded her arms.

"Okay," I said and held my wrists out toward her while she eyed me suspiciously.

"Damn, little girl. You love your dad so much that you are willing to take the fall for him?" She reached for her handcuffs.

I backed up. "Wait…what?" I asked for clarification and returned my wrists back to my side.

"Look…I been looking for Lucifer for five years, ever since he busted out of prison. We were on to him, but he went underground, and we hit a wall until we got a tip this morning that you were here in Ann Arbor. I'm willing to forgive that little mishap at the hospital since nobody got hurt, as long as you help me out with finding your father." She rubbed her weary eyes.

I took heed to everything she was saying. I was elated to know that she thought my daddy was the real LB, but the fact that she said she was given a tip about our whereabouts raised concern for me. "Agent Nichols, I haven't seen my father since that night of the shootout at the hospital. Matter of fact, I been hiding from him all this time, so I'm not sure how I can help you. Just out of curiosity though, where did you get this tip about us being here?"

"Well truth be told, I caught the news broadcast this afternoon announcing the AMBER alert for Candace's daughter, DeShawna. It was reported that she was abducted from the school bus this morning. When they revealed the mother's name, I was unsure, but when they flashed the picture of the two of them playing, I knew right off that it was her, and if I could find her, you two wouldn't be too far away. Now I see my hunch was right." She nodded at White Girl and pulled out a Newport and lit it.

"So how can we help you Nichols, if we ain't seen Lucifer in five years?" Maine asked.

"That's up to you two. All I know is that I retire in two weeks, and before I go I want that bastard's head." She slid her hand across her neck, signaling a cut throat motion.

"Look ma'am…right now we have other things to deal with, starting with this little situation with my daughter," White Girl cut in.

"Listen White Girl—can I call you that?"

White Girl nodded.

"I hope your baby girl is alive and well—I really do—but I've been chasing this asshole for most of my career with the Bureau, and I ain't leaving here without one of two things. Either I'm taking Lovely and Jermaine with me—and maybe even you for your involvement in this case—or else I need an agreement to help me find that son-of-a-bitch." She rolled her eyes and blew smoke.

I couldn't believe everything was going down at once. I wanted my niece back home and safe, but I couldn't save her if I was locked up; however, I damn sure wasn't ready to go looking for trouble with Lucifer.

"Hello! Are you listening?" Nichols snapped her fingers.

"What up?" I asked.

"I said I ain't got all day, so what did you decide? I mean, if you're too scared to go after the person who killed your mother and your innocent fourteen-year-old sister, I understand. It's easy enough to have a squad car escort you to your destiny."

As she mentioned what that bastard did to my baby sister, I remembered how he had not one shred of remorse, and I came to the conclusion that it was about to be on and poppin'. "I'm in," I added before I had a second thought.

She smiled.

"What about DeShawna, L? How you gon' go after Lucifer for this Fed and still help me get my baby back?" White Girl questioned.

"I got you, and you know this," I answered.

"So we got ourselves a deal then?" The agent put her hand out for a shake.

I ignored it but nodded my head in agreement.

"All right. Son, let's get outta here so these ladies can get busy." She grabbed Maine's handcuffed wrists and turned to walk away.

"Yo! What the fuck is up?" he asked before I could.

"Look, I've got to take one of you in so my superiors ain't riding my ass, but once this thing gets settled, I swear on my daughter's life I will let you out. Hell, I'll personally escort you back home. I'm sorry, but there is no way around it. That's just the way it is." She nodded at the other agents standing at the end of my driveway.

"Maine, I can't do this without you," I started to complain, but he shushed me.

"Look Ma, you got to! Ain't no other way. We need Shawnie back, and we need Lucifer gone so we can get on with our lives, a'ight? I'ma hold this thing down, and you do the same, Ma. We got two weeks. I will be in touch." He winked at me.

I ran up to him and kissed him on the cheek.
"You got this, Lovely. I know you do."

CHAPTER 12

It had been hours since Maine was taken into custody, and I was having *déjà vu* because the scene seemed all too familiar as me and White Girl paced the floor to devise a plan to get Shawnie back. The last time we had done that was when Tori was shot. The only difference this time was that my brother Do It wasn't there.

"Fuck, man L. We can't do this shit," she said as she stopped to take a swig of the Hennessy bottle she had been nursing for two hours. She was wasted, but what could I say? Her baby was gone, and I could only imagine how that would feel to a mother.

"White Girl, why don't you lie down while I figure this out, boo?"

"Naw, fuck that L. That's my baby out there in those cold streets all alone. Ya' feel me?" she slurred.

"Yeah girl, I feel you." I comforted her as she began to cry well into the night.

* * *

It was almost five in the morning before she finally went to sleep, and when she did, I went straight back to the drawing board. By nine that morning, I had come up with a game plan to satisfy everyone, but first I needed to hit the streets for some money for fucking Frankie. I looked through the whole house, and the few thousand I found was nowhere near the millions I needed. Maine didn't like keeping large sums of cash in the house, and he never understood why niggas put their whole life savings in one place instead of spreading it out. He said, "If you was ever robbed or raided, your shit would be toast, and you'd be back at damn square one."

I needed to get my day started with not an hour to lose, so I pulled out of the driveway in my ash-gray Porsche truck and headed straight for downtown Detroit, calling Coco in the process.

"Hey Leslie," she answered.

"Coco it's me, Lovely," I said.

"Um..." she stuttered hesitantly.

"Look...there's no more hiding, baby. I'm back, and I will be there in an hour and a half. Call Tiny and find Meechie for me."

"For real?" she questioned.

"Damn straight. This is the real deal, Holyfield!" I gripped the steering wheel tighter as the adrenaline began to flow.

"All right," she said and hung up.

* * *

I got out of my truck and walked up to the door of Salon 3k, her beauty shop. I must admit it felt good to be back in the heart of the city.

Coco must've spotted me when I pulled up, because she emerged from the doors and damn near tackled me to the ground. "What's up, bestie? What the hell happened yesterday? You never called me."

"Girl I will explain everything shortly," I said, holding back the anger that threatened to escape at any second, I was on one for real.

We walked into the shop, and there was Tiny, my girl from back in the day—a real get-money bitch who I kept on my team for odd jobs and hustles. She knew every and anybody this side of the world. "Girl. I thought you were dead!" She shook her head and gave me a tight hug.

"Damn so did I!" I heard from behind me. It was Meechie, the man who held my drug operation down when I was LB. Even though he'd worked for my pathetic father years back, I knew Meechie was a stand-up guy and could always be trusted.

I reached up for a hug.

"So sorry to hear about Do It, for real!" He squeezed tight, and the tears began to fall.

"I know man. That's fucked up what happened to my brother, but I'm going to find out who did that shit and avenge his death. Believe that!" I broke the embrace and wiped my eyes. "That's part of the reason I'm here."

"What's good Ma?" he asked as Tiny listened intently and Coco locked the door to her shop so no one else could enter.

"Me, White Girl, and Maine been lying low all this time, and I thought shit was velvet, but yesterday, Do It's daughter Shawnie was kidnapped right off the school bus. When I got home, there was a note from Frankie saying, 'a niece for a nephew'!" They gasped, and I continued, "He left his number. When I called, the person on the phone said Frankie wants six million dollars and LB, or else bad things are gonna happen to Shawnie. Maine went to the bank to get the money, but the Feds snatched him, and one of the agents basically told me that if she don't have LB in two weeks, then Maine and me are going down for everything—even Tori's murder."

"Damn," Meechie chimed in, shocked.

"So what you need us to do girl? You know I got your back," Tiny added, just as I knew she would.

"Yeah, we're all ready to play our parts," Coco agreed.

"Well Meechie, Maine's accounts are frozen and we only had a few thousand stashed around the house. I need you to find us some licks to hit so I can get this money to Frankie—not to mention guns and all. As soon as Maine is released, I'll shoot you the cash back. You know I'm good for it."

He nodded his understanding, took out his phone and got got busy right away.

"Tiny I need you to put word on the street that Lovely Brown is back, on a mission to find Lucifer's sorry ass. I also want you to plan the biggest welcome-home party for me, complete with invites, radio time, and hell, even a commercial if you have to. Coco you know I would never put you in this unless I had to, and this time I have to boo."

"Lovely you are my bitch till the world blow, so you know I got your back. I owe you so much, and I'm thankful for you getting me this salon and taking me up out those strip clubs. Like I said girl, no matter what it is, I got you."

"Girl the salon was nothing. You know if I got it, then you do too. The only thing I need from you right now is a place to stay."

"That's it?" she quizzed.

"Yep, that's it. Oh…and you spread the word on my return to your clients and stuff. We both know all them girls that come here definitely got a man in the game. I want to make sure this information get to the right people, if you know what I mean."

"Cool. So when is the party supposed to happen?"

"We got two weeks," I answered, just as Meechie got off the phone.

"All right. I got something set up for tonight then. We need to get started as soon as possible. You game?" he asked.

"Yeah. What's the info?" I sat down in one of the burnt orange chairs in the lobby of the salon, and he sat next to me.

Coco took Tiny in the back, and then Meechie went into details.

"There is a big money drop-off going down tonight at midnight on Chalmers. This nigga called Scoot been rolling heavy, and right now he's the man on the East Side. My dog just told me there are two men in the house, strapped and ready to pop a nigga that dares to snatch they shit. Another dude goes to pick up, and there are two men in the van—one a driver and the other in the back with the money."

"What's the expected payout?" I jumped in.

"About two million," he answered.

My mouth dropped. "Square biz?" I confirmed. I definitely didn't expect so much of a take in one night, but I wasn't complaining.

"Yeah. This nigga I did a bid with way back in the day is our connect on this, and if all goes to plan, I told him we'd toss him $400,000. Cool?"

"Hell yeah, that's cool. Who is doing this with us, and what's their cut?" I asked, knowing that everyone came at a price—and sometimes a heavy one.

"Just me, you, and White Girl if she up to it. No cuts. All this shit goes to getting lil mama back." He stood from his seat.

I shook my head. "No my nigga. You got to take a cut. That's only fair."

"Yo, I'm good. Believe that. When I worked for you, you left a nigga right and I ain't never forgot that! Plus, yo' whack-ass father need to be merked for that shit he pulled with his own family."

I couldn't have agreed more. It was time somebody took Lucifer out.

We finished our plans and dapped fists. Meechie left, and I told Coco I would be back shortly.

"Where are you going?"

"Just to check on a few things, but I will see you later." I threw up the deuces and got into my truck. I grabbed my cell phone and called White Girl.

"Hello," she answered in a whisper.

"Do you have a hangover?" I laughed.

"Hell yeah, but why you leave me?"

"Girl your ass wasn't trying to wake up, so I had to do what I had to do. When you finally get up and ready, meet me down here in Detroit. I spoke with some people, and we got something to take care of." I spoke in code because anybody could have been listening.

"Okay. I'm 'bout to shower now. Where do you want to meet?"

I heard her stirring in the bed. "Call me later, and I will tell you," I said, ending the call.

CHAPTER 13

I pulled off and merged onto I-75 from Jefferson and made my way over to my old house in Southfield. As I pulled up, I had to think about going inside. The last time I was there, me and Do It were together, on our way out to pick up the money from Frankie's nephew. I wished I could've seen the future and just headed in the opposite direction, but I couldn't. Now I needed to go inside and look for any money we may have left behind in our mad dash to flee the place.

I stepped out of the truck and put on my Fendi sunglasses to block the sun and part of my appearance from those that might be looking a little too hard.

"Are you looking to buy the place?" an old white woman asked from my left. She looked like Betty White, standing there with a drippy garden hose.

"Huh?" I said, turning to face her.

She walked over to me. "You might not want that house," she leaned in and whispered.

"Why not?" I asked out of mere curiosity.

"Well, I heard the young people who used to live there were into drugs or something of that nature, and it's been raided several times." Her eyes widened as she told me the gossip.

"Really? How long ago was the last raid?" I questioned.

"It's true. It sent all the neighbors up in a tizzy, but I believe the last raid was maybe three or four years ago or so." She blocked her eyes from the sun with her gaudy green garden glove.

"Was it the police that raided the house?" My mind wondered why the house was raided so much, especially three or four years after we were already long gone.

"Well now, that I don't know, but I do know that every time it happens, it's always at night. Now that you mention it, I've never seen any police cars, and nobody was wearing a badge." She looked stumped.

"So no one has been inside recently?" I confirmed, just in case I needed to go back to the truck and retrieve my nine millimeter from my secret compartment in the passenger seat.

"From time to time, a couple squats there. The man is in a wheelchair. But I haven't seen those folks in about a month or so."

"Jessie, get back over here and stop meddling in other folks' business! Ya' hear me?" a bossy old man called from the front door of the lady's ranch-style house.

"Coming!" she replied to him. "Listen, you be careful going in there, okay?" she said to me before she practically ran into her house.

I went back to my truck and grabbed my gun, just in case. I turned the key, which still worked, and walked inside. I checked every room and even went down in the basement. I was alone, but someone had surely been there. In the living room I found old newspaper clippings about the breakout of Lucifer, the shootout at the hospital, and even the death of Kierra. I was totally puzzled, but I couldn't stop and dwell on it right then, so I went into Do It and White Girl's old room to see if they left any money or guns behind. I found nothing but various pictures scattered around. Every inch of wall and morsel of carpet was completely destroyed. The same went for my room and the room I made for Tori, even though she never got a chance to see it.

I remembered that I had hidden some money in the garage under a loose concrete slab. I hadn't told anyone about it, so I had to wonder if it was still there. I went out the backdoor and into the garage. I grabbed an old steel pipe that was resting against the wall and began to search for the loose slab. I was on the fourth concrete square when I felt it wobble, so I pushed the steel pipe down up against the concrete to move it, and it finally gave about five attempts later. I dropped to my knees and began to claw at the dirt until my fingertips rested against something plastic. I pulled with all my strength, and the bag slid out with ease. I untied the bag and saw a satisfying amount of money, but I decided to count it later. I closed the bag and headed out of the garage. After I got in my truck and pulled off, I waved goodbye to Jessie, who was back outside in her yard, planting some flowers.

CHAPTER 14

"Hey it's me. Where are you?" White Girl asked before I even had a chance to say hello.

"I'm headed to Coco's crib. Meet me there," I answered.

"Is she still in the projects?" she asked.

I laughed because that was really a good question that I had not a clue about. "I'm not sure. Hold on and let me call her on three-way." I clicked over, dialed Coco's number, and clicked back over to White Girl just as Coco answered.

"What up, doe?"

"Hey, me and White Girl are on the phone, and we need to know if your ghetto ass is still staying in the PJs?" We laughed in unison because my girl was a true project chick—a PJC all the way. Her whole family lived there, and she vowed she would live there, too, as long as her rent stayed under a hundred a month.

"Ladies you know the projects are in my blood, but they put me out." She laughed.

"What! Are you serious? Why?" White Girl questioned.

"After the salon opened up, my money grew, and with the kind of income I get from Salon 3k, I had to go. But it's cool. My mom, aunts, and grandma are still there, so I visit every day."

"Well where do you live now, because we are on the way over there? Are you home yet?" I asked.

"Well right now I'm actually with my new man. I want you guys to meet him, and I can be on my way home now," she said, and I could tell she was smiling.

"Damn! Don't let us interrupt. Me and L can get a hotel downtown and catch yo' freaky ass tomorrow," White Girl said.

Coco smacked her lips. "Whatever, bitch. You know y'all ain't interrupting, but anyway, I'm over there off of Chene, at those new suites they just put up off the river. You'll see the new construction sign." She rattled off her address, and I put it in the GPS.

Her place was twenty-three minutes away, and I pulled up five minutes before White Girl, who was driving her pink 300.

"Hey, I brought some shit from the house just in case we need it." She grabbed two duffel bags from the trunk and handed one to me.

"Damn. The neighbors will think I'm rich with these expensive cars out here putting my lil Altima to shame," Coco said and hugged White Girl.

"Where are my godkids?" I asked. I had not seen Cory or Cornell in a very long time and I truly missed them.

"Girl they're still with their dad. He called me at your house, talking about Cornell was so sick. That nigga thought I was going to just say to bring them home, but I took some medicine over to his house and kept it moving. Shit, I need a damn break! Cory ass is bad as hell and Cornell is spoiled as hell. Zo ain't getting off that easy."

"What's he sick with?" White Girl asked.

"Girl I didn't even ask, but I dropped off cold medicine, allergy medicine, headache medicine, diarrhea, and constipation medicine…shoot, the boy will live with whatever he got," Coco said with a laugh..

"They can't be that bad for real, Coco. How is my nigga Zo?" I asked about her baby daddy and her on-again/off-again play thing.

"Shit! The last time you seen them, they were cute, just six and four. Now they some bad-ass nine- and seven-year-olds. Zo is all right...still working my nerve about getting married, but he can't stop fucking dem hoes."

I just shook my head. It was never ending with them.

"So you got two marriage proposals?" White Girl asked.

"You know how I do it." She popped the invisible collar on her orange halter top. "Let's go in the house. My mama sent a little somethin'-somethin' over here for y'all," she smirked.

My mouth watered instantly. Coco's mama could throw down on some soul food.

"I sure hope it's something deep fried. Lord knows I love that woman's chicken."

White Girl followed us inside the stylish but modest home. Her walls were painted a very tan brown and were trimmed in dark chocolate. Her hardwood floors glistened, and her cathedral ceiling with two skylights gave the place a nice architectural design.

"You know my mama sent over her famous fried chicken, macaroni and cheese, collard greens, and that hot-ass jalapeño bread she makes." She began to lift the lids off the Styrofoam containers.

"Let me wash my hands, girl. I can't wait to dig in," I said, as White Girl damn near knocked me down.

CHAPTER 15

"That was so good!" I said just as my cell phone rang. "Hello?"

"You have a collect call from…" a computerized voice began.

"Maine," my man's voice said.

"Press one to except, or simply hang up if you do not wish to receive this call."

I pressed one. "Baby, are you okay?"

"Come on L. You know a nigga is 100. Y'all cool? Is a plan in motion yet?"

I smiled as the visual of my sexy future husband crossed my mind. "Yeah boo. We're in Detroit now, and everything is good. I will have you home in no time," I reassured him.

"I ain't worried 'bout me. Just get my lil Shawnie back home."

"I will baby," I said, and we ended the call. It was right then that I remembered I had the bag of money in my truck. "Oh shit. I'll be right back," I announced. I went outside and returned shortly with the huge black garbage bag. I set it down on the living room floor.

"What's that?" Coco asked.

"Money that I had stashed away at the old house." I untied the bag and emptied it. We all watched as bills hit the floor, some old and wrinkled, and others crisp and new. "Y'all grab some, and let's count it," I said. I sat on the floor and slid a pile my way; my friends did the same, and the count was over in no time.

"Damn! We got $450,000 here." White girl pointed at the several stacks of money that were now sitting neatly on top of the table.

"Damn right! Now that's some shit to smoke to." Coco reached in her ashtray and pulled out a half-smoked blunt.

"Girl you been smoking weed since you were what, thirteen? You've probably puffed every type of weed out there. When you going to quit? " I stood from the floor and stretched. My friend was a true weed head, and it was part of her character.

"With all the shit you been through lately, I'm shocked you ain't started."

We all laughed at that one; the Lord knew it was true.

"Lovely ain't smoking shit, so pass the bud this way." White Girl extended her hand and I flipped them both the middle finger.

"I'm about to go upstairs and get changed for this thing with Meechie. He texted me and said he would be here in thirty minutes."

"You still ain't said what we doing yet." White Girl choked on the blunt and passed it back to Coco.

"I will tell you in the car," I said and ran up the stairs. I never went into details around Coco because I didn't want her to go to jail for knowing too much. She was a ghetto girl, but real street life wasn't her thing. Plus she needed to be around for my godsons. It was for her own good, and she understood my reasons, so she never gave me flack about leaving her out of certain conversations.

I threw on a pair of black Juicy Couture sweats, a black wife-beater, a matching jacket, and finished it off with my black Reeboks and black Detroit baseball hat.

White Girl came into the room we would be sharing and tossed her overnight bag on top of the twin-sized mattress on her side of the room. She unzipped it and pulled out a pair of dark blue Aéropostale velour pants with a matching long-sleeved t-shirt, and a pair of blue and black Nikes. Her long blonde hair was braided back in two French braids; Coco must've just done it like that since it wasn't that way when I had first gone upstairs. After she finished tying up her shoes, she tossed me two guns out of the second bag and placed two others in the holster that she had just put on her back.

The door bell rang, and we both looked at each other, knowing it was on.

"Lovely, Meechie is here!" Coco shouted up the stairs.

On my way out of the room, White Girl grabbed me in an embrace. "We got to get her back L. She is all that I have!"

"We will…or I will die trying," I said, and with that we exited the room.

CHAPTER 16

It was half-past midnight, the time when we were told the drop would be made. I was nervous as hell.

"What the fuck is the holdup?" White Girl pounded her fist into the back of Meechie's seat.

"Chill, shortie. He's coming. Just be patient," he answered.

While we sat on the corner a few houses away from where the drop was happening, we spotted a man coming out of the house several times, looking down the street. My guess was that they were waiting on the truck as well and had no idea where it was. We waited in silence for about fifteen more minutes, and then it was show time.

"Yo! There they go," Meechie pointed out.

We jumped out of the old school, masked, with our guns out. We ran up behind the man who was just reaching for the back door of the truck to get the money.

"Stick up, bitch!" White Girl said with her pistol aimed right at the back of his head.

"You got it, Ma!" He put his hands up.

The back door to the truck opened, and there was a gunman locked, loaded, and ready to shoot, but we were expecting him.

Meechie took him down with a bullet to the knee.

"Aw, shit!" he hollered as he fell from the truck, dropping his gun to ground.

I picked up the weapon just in time to see the second man emerging from the house, letting off rounds in the dark.

POP!

I barely missed one as I fell on the side of a black Marauder that was parked in front of their house. I looked up at Meechie, who was shooting back, and then down at White Girl, who was trying to cuff the men on the ground with zip-ties as she dodged the spray of bullets. I crawled around the car and ended up behind the gunman. "Drop that fucking gun, or you're dead!"

"Do you know who the fuck you're messing with?" he asked.

"No and I really don't give a fuck!" I answered. I reached for his gun with my gloved hand and placed it behind my back. I jerked a bit because it was so hot that it burned a little.

"Bitch you might as well kill me, because if you don't, I will find you, and I won't hesitate to pull the trigger." He spat on the ground.

"Not a problem," White Girl answered. She walked up to him and pulled the trigger, blowing brain matter all over the place, including my clothes.

I almost gagged, especially when Meechie took his gun and did the same to the guys on the ground.

"Grab this fucking money and let's roll!" he barked.

"Shit, my nigga! You wasn't supposed to kill them and leave me alive. That shit will make me look suspect like a muthafucka. Just give me my cut, and I'm out! I need to catch the next thing smoking out of this place." Our contact rubbed his hands together with a greedy look on his face.

Meechie reached into one of the bags he was holding. "I got you my nigga."

BANG! BANG!

What Meechie gave him for a cut was two to the head, and I watched his lifeless body drop to the concrete.

All in all, we carried about twenty bags back to the old school, and within minutes we were back on our way.

"What the fuck was that?" I asked White Girl as I pointed down at my brain-splattered jacket.

"That was how you get shit done, Lovely! When a muthafucka tell you to kill them, then your ass better kill them!"

"And Meechie you didn't tell me you were going to go along with that plan," I snapped.

"Look shortie, shit got out of hand and went sideways, but we needed that money and we got it—all of it. It is what it is, Ma." He rolled his mask up and gave me an apologetic nod.

"Fuck!" I spat and hit the dashboard. I was pissed, and I wasn't trying to hide it.

"Just calm down. It's over now. What's done is done, and there ain't shit we can do to change things, all right?" Meechie pulled into an alleyway and cut the car off.

"What's up?" White Girl asked.

"We're 'bout to hop in the whip with my lady and burn this muthafucka," he answered.

Sure enough, some chick in a White Nissan pulled up.

Meechie walked over to the car and came back with a duffel bag in his hand. "Put this on." He tossed me and White Girl a pair of sweats and a wife-beater. "Give me the other ones."

Me and White Girl did as we were told and then helped Meechie move the money to the Nissan. I watched as he poured gasoline all over the car and inside it, then he threw a cigarette to ignite the flame. We sped off, but I could still see it burning in the distance.

"Yo, I'm going to stash this shit. You girls get some sleep, cuz we got more work coming in a day or two," he said as we pulled in front of Coco's door.

I was still pissed, so I got out and said nothing. I opened the door, not knowing that it would close on its own, damn near letting it smack White Girl in her face.

"Damn girl! Get your panties out your ass!" She stretched her hand out just before it hit her.

"Don't say shit to me right now." I took my shoes off and ran up the stairs with her high yellow ass on my heels.

"I can't believe you're really mad at me for saving your ass! That nigga said he was going to kill you. Do you understand what that means?"

She put her finger in my face, and I smacked it away. "Get your goddamn finger out of my muthafuckin' face!" I snapped as she tried me again. Just as she tried the third time. I socked her ass right in the mouth. "Yo' ass just wanted to keep testing me, didn't you?" I pulled my gun out from my waist and put it to her head. "Is this gangsta enough, bitch?" I asked.

"For real? It's like that?" She stared back at me.

"Yeah. It's like that if you ever fuckin' try me again. Just because I ain't blowing niggas' brains out don't mean I ain't gangsta," I spat as Coco ran into the room.

"Lovely, put the gun down boo," she requested, and I did. "What the fuck happened?"

"I guess it's just two bad bitches having one fucked-up night!" White Girl answered and walked out of the room.

"Lovely, what's the matter?" she asked, rubbing my back, and I wished I could tell her, but I couldn't. I just asked for some private time, and she obliged. I sat down on the bed and prayed for forgiveness. I understood the streets and their ways, but killing people who didn't deserve it just never sat well with me. I knew every action had a consequence, and because I didn't know who killed my baby sister, I ended up going after the wrong person. I took his life because of it, and truthfully, I never forgave myself for that. Those somewhat innocent men who lost their lives that night were a reminder of what street life does to people. I thought about Tori and DeShawna and what people like Meechie, White Girl, and ultimately me were doing to the innocent. *They don't deserve this!*

* * *

Morning came, and I woke up to White Girl sitting on her bed looking at me. "What?" I asked.

"Listen, I just want to apologize for last night. I thought I was doing a good thing, but I thought about it over and over, and I can see why you got upset with me." She got up and walked over to sit on my bed.

"Look, I understand you were looking out for me, and I appreciate that and all, but that's how niggas go to jail. One bad decision, and you turned our 'hood robbery—which no law enforcement would care about—into a quadruple homicide in the middle of a residential area."

"Damn. I didn't look at it like that. You are my family, and I only know to protect the people I love." She put her arm around my shoulder.

"You are my family too, and we do have to protect each other—just not like that unless it is absolutely necessary. I might already be catching a case, and I don't need no murders added to my files." I stood and stretched.

After we hugged, we went downstairs to kick it with Coco before she left for work. "The dead have risen," she remarked as we entered her kitchen.

"Shut up. Where is breakfast?" I teased.

"Well the only breakfast we have today is bagels and cream cheese, but I do have a surprise for you all." She smiled and pointed to the living room, and we walked over there. "Manicures, pedicures, hair, and make-up!" she exclaimed. Coco had her living room set up like a beauty salon, like she was bringing Salon 3k home to us.

"Aw, thanks girl, but did my shit look that bad." I rubbed at my ponytailed hair.

"Yeah boo. You need a little attention, and so do you White Girl. Damn! Ann Arbor must not have no beauty shops." She laughed, and so did the nail tech and make-up artists who were set up at their stations in the living room.

"Fuck you!" White Girl said, and I made the same gesture with my finger.

"I'm Wanda," announced the make-up artist, a heavyset Angie Stone-looking woman.

I smiled at her.

"Lovely, girl you know me!" The nail tech, Meka, jumped up and gave me a tight hug.

"Wassup, Meka? What's been going on girl?" I sat down at her station and began to chat while she did my nails.

White Girl followed Coco into the kitchen to get her hair washed. Coco had just dyed it the other day, but she was going to do it big today since she had all of her products.

"Girl, same-ole, same-ole. You know…different day, same shit. I heard about Do It, and I wanted you to know I'm sorry for your loss. Girl I thought they got you too when you didn't show up to the funeral, but I'm glad you're back," she said as she filed my nails down.

"Yeah, for obvious reasons, I couldn't come back. Anyway, how was it?" I asked, staring intently as she turned my nails to dust with her file.

"It was real nice girl, even though he had a closed casket. They said his face was unrecognizable, so they had to do it that way, but shit over 500 people still showed up." She moved on to buffing.

"Do you know who was in charge of the funeral?" I asked, my mind racing.

"Nope. Don't know about that, but Swift had the body. I'm sure they would know."

I picked out a peach color polish, and she began to paint my nails with it. I made a mental note to check in with Swift Funeral Home as soon as I got a free moment; the whole closed casket business made me uneasy. Something was off about it, even if I couldn't quite put my finger on it.

"Girl did you hear about that homicide over there by June Bug and them?" Wanda asked Meka.

"No. The news is too damn depressing to watch, so I didn't see it," she answered.

"Girl, they said four men was murdered right outside the trap house. Two of them niggas was cops," Wanda added.

I almost pissed myself right then and there when I heard that, but I regained my composure and asked, "Do they have any leads?"

"Not yet, but they said the hit looked professional."

"All right. You're next," Coco said, snapping me out of my trance. She put White Girl under the dryer as I shuffled across the wood floor, not wanting to damage my matching peach pedicure. She had all the hair care products laid out on the counter, and I bent down to put my head under the running water. Her hands felt awesome against my scalp, and I relaxed. Letting the moment take control of my thoughts, I soon began thinking about Do It and about what happened last night. I almost fell asleep as she blow-dried and then pressed my newly copper-brown hair. "All right, babe. You're all set. Go and let Wanda do your make-up." She gave me a hand mirror to look at myself.

I shook my lengthy hair from side to side. I loved the way Coco pressed hair, and she'd definitely gotten better over the years. "I don't really think I need make-up. I ain't doing much today but making some runs," I said, trying to catch a pass so I could get to the funeral home.

"Bullshit. I need you to get make-up because Tiny set up a photo shoot for you today." She pushed me back into the living room, and I sat in Wanda's chair.

"What's the photo shoot for?"

"Your welcome home flyer...for your party. Remember?" She folded her arms.

"Oh yeah. I forgot," I said as Wanda got to work.

She finished about twenty minutes before the photographer arrived, and even after she'd packed up and left, I was still staring in the mirror admiring her work. White Girl had been spray-tanned and actually had a hint of color to herself, so she was admiring her own reflection too.

"Come on in, Dontay. Hey Tiny," Coco said from the front door.

"Wassup, bitches!" She ran into the room and gave me a hug, dapping up White Girl on her way in.

"Girl, a photo shoot? For real?" I said.

"Yeah, for real. Hell you said you wanted everyone to know about the party, and this is how you do it. I also have radio spot for you in a few days, so get your sexy voice together."

"My voice is always sexy," I shot back, and then we got right down to business. She had brought a gold cat-suit trimmed in rhinestones. It was very revealing, but I loved it. It was perfect for the theme of the party; Tiny called it "Diamonds and Gold: A Baller's Ball to Welcome Home one of Detroit's Finest."

CHAPTER 17

After the photo shoot, we all went out to a late lunch at the Thai House. I wanted to tell White Girl the 411, but we really didn't get another moment alone, and as soon as lunch was over, I had to dip, because I got a call from Meechie telling me to meet him—alone. "What's the deal?" I asked as I pulled alongside him on Whitcomb and Six Mile in the parking lot of the liquor store.

"Yo. First off, I wanted to say my bad for last night," he said.

"Like you said, we can't change it, so it's whatever," I answered.

"Second, I wanted to tell you that your girl is buggin'." He lit a Black & Mild.

"White Girl?" I asked for clarification.

"Yeah, her. She called me a little while ago asking me to meet her and give her the money so she could stash it—"

"What?" I cut him off.

"That's what I'm saying! I know it's her kid we saving and all, but I don't get a good vibe from her; and then she was trying to go into detail on the phone and shit—like, 'Meechie, we had to dead dem niggas, didn't we?' and shit like that. I'm staring at the phone because I know she know better." He flicked the Black & Mild out into the air.

"What the fuck is going on?" I said out loud, more to myself than to him.

"That's what I'm sayin', my nigga. Her and Do It was my peoples, but you need to watch her." He scratched his bald head.

"Yeah, that's real talk, but did you hear that the niggas y'all merked last night was undercover officers?" I asked.

The crazy expression he gave me told me he didn't know. "Get the fuck out of here!" He scratched his head again.

I nodded. "Look…what's done is done now, and you burned everything linking us to that shit in that car—so we should be good."

He lit a Newport cigarette to chase the high he just got off his blunt. "Anyway, tonight we gon' hit these low-key niggas over at the motel on west Eight Mile. I was in the barbershop getting my face trimmed up, and this nigga was in there bragging that him and his partner hit a lick at one of the casinos out of state and cashed the chips in another casino here. I don't know how much they got, but we need whatever it is. Don't bring your girl—jus' me and you, and on my word, there ain't gon' be no trigger action unless we have to." I agreed, and he walked back to his car as I nodded at him.

"I'll be ready when you call!" I said and got back into the truck with even more on my mind than when I woke up that morning, like why White Girl was calling Meechie on some other stuff. I had nowhere to be for a while, so I took it as the perfect opportunity to go to Swift and see what the deal was about my brother's closed casket.

* * *

Just as I pulled up in the parking lot, my cell rang. "Hello?" I answered.

"Auntie L, when are you coming to get me?" DeShawna's little voice asked.

"Oh my God! Shawnie, are you okay baby?"

"Yes Auntie L, but I'm scared and I want to come home."

"I swear, baby, you'll be home soon. I promise," I said just as one of Frankie's goons got on the phone.

"How are you coming with the money?"

"I still have until next week, right?" I snapped.

"I will be in touch...and you better not make me wait a moment past then." *Click.*

I exhaled and regained my composure. I got out of my truck and walked inside the creepy-ass white funeral home.

"Hello Miss. May I help you?" an older beauty asked as she approached me in a form-fitting black and white Chanel dress. I smiled as she extended her perfectly manicured hand my way. The woman reminded me a lot of Diane Carroll.

"Yes ma'am." I cleared my throat. "My brother Dashawn was—" I was startled as the sound of the door behind me burst open, slamming up against the wall.

"Maybelle, he's gone! My dearly beloved husband is gone girl, and I need your help!" another older woman cried as she brushed past me, collapsing in the arms of the Diane Carroll look-a-like.

"Not Eddie? Frances, I know Eddie hasn't left here to be with the Lord just yet," Maybelle shot back, seeming just as upset as the intruder, who looked like the mother on that old *Good Times* TV show.

"Oh, Lawd!" she screamed, and I stepped back.

"Now Frances, just calm down. Take these Kleenex and go into my office. I will be with you directly." Maybelle grabbed the box of tissue off the lamp table and passed it to the distraught woman. Looking up at me with an apologetic expression, she added, "I'm so sorry, dear. I am the only one here tonight. Eddie is my brother-in-law, and Frances is my sister. I have to tend to her now, but will you please come back another day?"

I simply nodded and turned on my heels to face the door.

* * *

I was a little disappointed that I couldn't get my answers right away, but maybe it was a good thing, because I really wasn't ready for my thoughts to be confirmed with a death certificate and possibly an urn to solidify things. I headed back to Coco's.

"Where you been?" White Girl asked as I walked into the house.

"Minding my business and leaving yours alone," I half-joked with a smile on my face.

"Whatever L." She flipped me the bird.

I set my purse down on the coffee table and went in the kitchen to retrieve a bottle of water. "Where is Coco?" I questioned.

"She said she had to go and do an important client at her house before some event tonight. I think she said ol' girl is a news anchor or something." White Girl tossed her Jet magazine aside and stood to stretch.

"Damn! My girl has blown up in the last five years," I said, feeling really proud.

"Hey. Can I ask you a quick question?"

"You just did," I joked.

"No, for real L. I'm serious," she said, and I could tell by the look on her face that she was.

"What's good?" I took a seat.

"I want you to promise me that if anything happens to me before we find my baby, you and Maine will look after her as your own." She wiped a tear away.

"Girl, ain't nothin' gon' happen to you. Believe that!" I replied as I began to feel really bad about not trusting her. As she continued to talk, my mind began to justify the things she had done earlier. I rationalized that as a mother, she just wanted to make sure the money that was going to be used to keep her daughter alive was safe and secure. I also came to the conclusion that she was just having an off moment when she was on the phone with Meechie. I knew without a shadow of a doubt that White Girl definitely understood never to discuss business on the phone. She had been drinking so much lately—her way of dealing with the pain of it all—so I made the executive decision not to tell her that Shawnie had called me. "I wish DeShawn was here L," she continued.

"Me too boo!" was all I could say, because the mention of him always got me choked up.

"I mean, why would this happen to the man of my dreams, huh? It could've been anyone in the world, but it was my man. We had just reconnected when I got out of jail, and I thought he was going to be my husband, but instead I'm a single mother of a child who's missing. This shit is just too much L. If it weren't for my baby, I would've checked out already—and now even she's gone." She sniffled.

White Girl and Do It had young love, but at sixteen, she ended up in jail after her mom's boyfriend, Poppy, told Narcotics that he thought she was selling cocaine. He was a hater. He already knew she was, but he wanted in and to have his cut, because she was damn good at it. That was how she got the name "White Girl," which was the street name for cocaine way before Jeezy made a song about it. They busted her with five ounces and offered her a plea deal if she told them who her supplier was or jail time if she didn't. Needless to say, she was true to the streets, so she ended up serving two years in juvie, and because of her assaults on various inmates and one corrections officer there, she got three more years tacked on to that.

"What do you mean, 'checked out'?" I turned toward her and wiped my face.

"L, I put my gun in my mouth plenty of nights, but then I thought about how selfish it would be to take another parent away from her."

"Listen…you know I know how you are feeling, but you have to keep pushing. Girl, in this game, souls get lost. That's just how this here goes down! I know the rules, and so do you. When shit gets to be too much, you just have to remove yourself from the situation." I shifted in my seat. "Maybe you should just fall back and let me and Meechie handle it."

"L, I know you mean well, but I can't just sit back and kick it like life is good while my baby girl is missing. You know that!" she snapped.

"I'm not trying to offend you, but to keep it 100, I feel like your judgment hasn't been up to par lately. I know you want Shawnie back, and so do I, but we won't get too far if somebody catch us slipping."

"So Meechie told you I was bugging earlier!" she stated more than asked.

"Huh?" I replied, dumbfounded because I honestly didn't know what else to say.

"I called him on some other shit earlier, and I was wrong to say what I said on the phone, but I just needed to know that the money was really protected."

"Yeah. He told me, and it's all good. Don't worry. Just be more careful. That shit we did last night is hot as hell."

"The block is hot over some 'hood niggas?" she quizzed.

"Them wasn't no 'hood niggas. They were undercover Narcotics officers, and we don't know if that shit was under surveillance or what, so just lie low for tonight, me and Meechie will handle everything." I stood.

"Please don't leave me out L," she pleaded.

I didn't know what else to say and was relieved that I didn't have to say anything because her cell phone rang, and she jumped up to retrieve it.

CHAPTER 18

It was around three in the morning when Meechie's text came through: *"See you in twenty."* I rubbed my eyes and blinked a few times to get my vision to cooperate. White Girl was sprawled out across her bed with an empty bottle of Hennessy at her bedside, which was normal for her lately. I grabbed my gym shoes and was out the door in five minutes. I noticed that Coco's car wasn't outside, so I called her to make sure she was okay.

"What's up, girl?" she whispered.

"You all right? Yo' ass ain't been home in a minute, so I'm just checking on you," I whispered, too, then laughed at myself because I had no idea why I was trying to keep my voice down.

"Girl I'm with my man. He's in the bathroom."

"I got to meet this so-called man since you keep on talking about him," I yawned.

"Yeah girl, you do…but I got to go, 'kay?" she said, and then the heifer had the nerve to hang up on my ass.

I turned on the radio to keep myself from dozing off again and was just in time to hear the commercial Tiny had put together for my welcome home party. It sounded super sexy, with all the hype music playing in the background. Immediately it made me crunk, not to mention that it sounded like a party nobody would want to miss. I knew the lines would be wrapped around the building—

just the way I wanted.

I pulled alongside Meechie, who was in a black Suburban this time. "What up, doe?" I asked after I rolled down my window

"Yo. Them niggas is in that room in the corner. Go park around back and then walk over here."

I did as I was told and was back in a flash. I scanned the old motel parking lot and noticed three cars: an old Buick, a Taurus, and a souped-up Cadillac Escalade, which had to belong to the men we were there to rob, because nobody with money would ever stay in a shithole like that. I shook my head at the stairs that led to the second level, where their room was located. "One way up and one way down. Damn!"

"Yeah I know, but it's all good. You knock on the door, and once they crack it, we bust in there lookin' like the police. He tossed me some gloves, a ski mask, a bulletproof vest, and a badge on a beaded chain.

"Damn nigga. You got all type of shit," I said as I put on my disguise.

"I been in this game for a long time, shortie. I always come prepared for any and every situation." He slid on his gloves.

"Yeah, your old ass should be a millionaire with all these jobs you pull." I knew Coco would have died at the sight of it, but I had to be practical, so I pulled my hair back into a ponytail because it was no time to be glamorous.

"I should, but like most knuckleheads out there, I was young and dumb, tricking and shit, you know!" He reminisced and then continued, "I messed up back then. I tried to save my son when he got in the game, but his ass was reckless."

"I didn't know you had a son, Meechie," I said as I pulled the badge over my neck.

"Yeah. His name was Isaac. He died around the time we got started with LB. Back then, me and you wasn't as close as we is now, so I didn't bother to say shit. You know me…ain't much for conversation."

"On my word Meechie, I really appreciate what you are doing for me. As soon as Maine is released and they unfreeze his assets, I will most definitely look out for you, old-timer."

"Girl I ain't hardly old! I'm only forty. I know you good peoples, and you always do the right thing, so this is on me. Now let's go."

He handed me a nickel-plated nine that looked identical to the personal legal one I always carried, except mine was inscribed *"Caution: Bad Bitch Behind the Trigger!"* I had it safely tucked behind my back just in case I ran out of ammo. I know it ain't smart to take your registered gun into a situation like that, but at the moment, I didn't have a spare. I'd rather have it and not need it than need it and not have it.

I led the way up the stairs, taking them two and three at a time, stretching my five-three frame to its limit. I peeked through a few windows where the nasty beige curtains had been left open and came to the conclusion that if the curtains were open, the rooms where vacant. Approaching the room in the corner, I looked back at Meechie, who walked with the calmness of someone who was just visiting a friend.

I tapped on the door.

"Who that?"

"You looking for some company?" I asked in my most seductive voice.

"Nigga, fuck that bitch. Don't open the door for that busto," I heard another voice chime in.

"I ain't no busto'. This is some classy pussy out here, Daddy… and I brought a friend. We ready for some hot shit if your paper is right," I spoke again in a sexy seductive tone. I was glad the rundown motel didn't have peepholes, or I would've been busted the moment they spotted my ski mask. I also took notice of the boarded-up window; it also could've blown our cover if it had been repaired and they were able to look through it.

I heard a muffled conversation between the two men on the

other side of the door, and then the door opened. A big, burly truck driver-looking man stood there. He towered over me at an even six feet.

I must admit I felt a little apprehensive, but a lady has to do what a lady has to do. "Get the fuck down on the ground and point me toward the money!" I shouted.

"Bitch, who da fuck you think you are?" The man tried to land a punch in my face, but I ducked, and he screamed in agony as his fist connected with the brick doorframe.

"I'm the police, muthafucka!" I spat. I put my gun to his face and backed him into the room.

"Fuck that!" I heard the second guy yell, and then I saw him searching up under the bed for something.

"Gun!" I screamed to Meechie, who was right on my heels.

POP! POP!

The second guy dropped down on the ground because Meechie had put two in his knees, and I knew we needed to get what we came for and get out, because with the gunfire, somebody might call the real cops.

"Big man, just show me where the cash at," I demanded.

"Bitch, your ass can't get shit but a stiff dick," he joked, grabbing his nasty nuts.

Before I knew it, I let a shot out right into his hand. I didn't know why I pulled the trigger, but was glad I did when I saw the revolver tucked into his drawers.

"Muthafucka!" he yelled.

"Now let's try this again, nigga. Where da bread at?"

"Fuck you, bitch!" He hocked up a wad of spit and hurled it in my direction.

I moved just before it connected with my body, but it still landed on my shoes. I was so pissed that I shot his ass again, this time in the leg, just for the hell of it—and I listened to him scream in pain.

"I will watch them while you look for the money," said

Meechie, who stood there with his pistol pointed.

I moved like a mad woman through the dirty-ass room. I was glad I had gloves on, because the tan carpet had all types of stains on it, and the wallpaper was dingy and peeling. I turned over the bed and the desk, but nothing was there. I went to the closet, but it was empty too. I peeked in the bathroom and pulled the shower curtain back and saw not one damn thing. I was stumped and began to think it was a waste of a trip and bullets, but then I heard a knock at the door. My heart pounded as I looked at Meechie, who was looking at the door with his gun still pointed at the two injured men. "Who is it?" I questioned in a whisper and then put the gun behind my back with the other one because I thought sure the police was there to respond to the gunshots. I don't know why I bothered hiding the guns, because it wouldn't matter once they saw the two men bleeding all over the place.

"You expecting somebody?" Meechie whispered to big man.

He wouldn't answer, so I went over there and lifted my leg, as if I was about to kick his wound.

He quickly nodded, "He got the money!"

Meechie turned the lights off and swung the door open while standing behind it.

"Bout' muthafucking time, bruh. I was starting to think something was up…OH SHIT!" the visitor said, backing out of the doorway. Meechie tried to reach for him, but the guy pulled away and ran toward the stairs, leaving three large suitcases at the door. He pulled a gun out of nowhere and fired in our direction.

"Shit!" I said, ducking a bullet while trying to pick up a suitcase. It was so heavy that I immediately dropped it.

Meechie leaned over the banister and let off a few shots to stop the man in his tracks, but it didn't work because he was moving like a track star. "Fuck! I'm out!" Meechie dropped his gun.

I reached down again to try to pick the suitcase up. I didn't care about old boy, as long as I got what I came for. I lifted the bag enough to drop it over the banister because there was no way we would get all three downstairs and to the car without making multiple trips.

Meechie reached behind my back, snatching my gun, and ran after the man who was still firing shots at us.

I tossed the other two suitcases over and then jumped over the banister behind the last one. It was only a second-floor drop, so it didn't hurt much. I got my bearings together and then stood up. There was money all over the ground because one of the suitcases had burst open. I tried to roll the two that were intact to my car. "Yo! Fuck dude. Let his ass go and grab this suitcase," I told Meechie over my shoulder.

Just as he came over to pick up the suitcase, a bullet hit the asphalt right next to me, and we both looked back.

"You blacks are forever tearing shit up, but I won't let you thugs destroy my shit!" an older Caucasian man said, standing there with a .22 pointed at us.

I assumed he was the owner and had come from the motel office after hearing the shootout between Meechie and the other guy.

"Old man, get back in your damn office like you never saw nothin'!" Meechie warned.

"Hell to the no! Your asses better be off of my property in five…four…three…two…" He let off a shot right into my arm.

Before I even had a chance to scream in pain, Meechie turned around and shot the man twice: once in the head and once in the chest.

I watched the man collapse and knew they'd have to find a new owner for the shitty motel. I looked down at my arm and began to feel flushed.

"You good ma'?" Meechie asked.

I nodded. I handed him the keys to my truck, and he loaded the suitcases up. I hopped into the passenger seat, and we sped off, burning rubber all the way down Eight Mile.

CHAPTER 19

"I can't believe your ass went and did that job without me!" White Girl snapped when I woke her up to help me patch up my arm.

"I don't need to hear that shit right now. Just help me out, all right?" I knew it was just a flesh wound, but it hurt like hell, and her complaining didn't make matters better. We went into the guest bathroom and found some towels, alcohol, and gauze. After I was bandaged up, I went down the hall into to Coco's bathroom and raided her medicine cabinet; all I could find was some weak-ass Tylenol. I headed back down the hall and stopped when I saw White Girl blocking the room door with her hands crossed.

"That was some shady shit L. I thought me and you was better than that."

"Listen…I told you earlier that you should just fall back, so this ain't no news to you." I rolled my eyes. The chick was really starting to bug me out.

"Something ain't right with your boy L," she shot as I walked past her.

I wanted to tell her that the feeling was mutual and that he thought the same about her, but I just kept my mouth closed.

She continued, "I was thinking earlier. Who in their right mind would go around taking all these huge risks and not ask for nothing in return? Square biz, I'm a nice person too, but even if it was my own damn mama asking for my help in a situation that required six million dollars, I'd be asking what my cut was—not to mention the fact that this nigga is taking the money from these jobs with him. For all we know, he could just be using our asses to get the money, and then be out. You ever thought of that? Hell, I bet even the money your ass got from tonight's job went with Meechie, didn't it?" She had the go-ahead and be honest look on her face.

I gladly burst her bubble. "For your information, not everybody has an ulterior motive. Some people look out for you on the strength of you and your pedigree. When he was riding with my drug business, you know I fed Meechie well…that nigga is like family! The money from tonight's job is downstairs. Would you like to come down and count it with me?" I headed back out of the room and down the stairs with her on my trails. When we got into the living room there were three large suitcases laid out on the living room floor; one was cracked open from being tossed over the balcony. "Any more questions?" I asked as I took a seat on the floor beside them.

"Where is Meechie?"

"Long story short, we ended up in a shootout." I pointed at my wounded arm and continued, "He had to leave the truck in the parking lot, and we jumped in my truck to get here. He brought the suitcases inside, and his friend picked him up to take him to dispose of the guns and go back to torch the Suburban."

"Y'all had a fucking shootout, and you tripped on me for popping a nigga?" She sat down on the floor with me.

"This was different. Somebody was actually shooting at us, so it had to be done. Anyway, enough about that. Let's count this money."

I was shocked when we hand counted a little over three million. I looked at the cable box, and it read 10:39 a.m. "Damn. We been counting for a little over four hours."

"My baby is almost home L! We just need a little more, and she is home free." White Girl danced around the money.

I was excited as well but too damn sleepy to do anything other than struggle with trying to bring one suitcase upstairs.

As I made it up the third step, Coco's front door burst open. "Hey, girl! What's that?" Coco asked as she closed the door behind her.

"Some heavy-ass money. Can you help me?" Between the wound on my arm and me being wiped out, I was lacking strength.

"Oh my God, Lovely! You been shot! Hey babe, let me call you back. I need to talk to my best friend." She blew a kiss into her Bluetooth and then snatched it out of her ear, placing it in her purse. "What the fuck happened?"

"You know I can't really go into details, but it's only a flesh wound. Don't worry."

"I can't leave your ass alone for one night without you coming back all shot up and shit. Damn." She smiled, and I laughed.

"I will be glad when all this is over, I swear," White Girl chimed in and I nodded in agreement.

"I know it's a fucked-up reason y'all had to come here, but truthfully, I am so happy to see y'all. L it's been five fucking years, girl, and them phone calls wasn't getting it! I have so much to catch you up on...like my new man De'Andre that you will meet real soon."

"Can you catch me up in a few hours, girl? I'm sleepy as hell!" I gave her an exasperated look.

She understood and didn't give me any flack.

We taped up the broken suitcase and took all three of them upstairs. Coco told us to hide them inside her attic, so that was exactly what we did. White Girl and I both crashed for what seemed to me like only five minutes, even though it was actually seven hours.

I awoke to the sound of my phone. "Hello," I mumbled. When

I heard the customary collect call message from jail, I immediately pressed one to accept the call.

"Baby what's good?" Maine's sexy, rough voice sent shivers through my body.

"Hey baby. How are you holding up?" I sat up in the bed and wiped sleep from eyes.

"You know I'm velvet. I keep telling you this ain't shit but a cakewalk for me. But how 'bout you boo? You holdin' it down?"

"Yeah. I been hitting a few spots, partying like crazy. I think I have to chill for a few days because them clubs be too damn hot!" I spoke in code, another way of telling him I'd hit a few licks and that shit was getting crazy and getting hot, so I was going to lay low for a day or two.

"Any word from that lil shortie?"

I knew he meant Shawnie. "Yeah. She sitting tight and told me everything's all good."

"Fo' sho. What about my old-school nigga from 'round the way? You heard from him yet?" he said, asking about my father.

"Not yet, but I'm sure I will real soon," I said as I made the bed up.

"Aye. Before I forget, have you collected the rent money yet? That shit is due soon, and I want to make sure you got enough," he asked about the six million I needed to retrieve our niece from Frankie and his goons.

"I got five forty-five, and—"

"Five minutes left on the call," interrupted the operator.

Maine sounded impressed that I had managed to get five million, four hundred fifty thousand in just a few days. Once all the business talk was behind us, we wasted the remaining time saying "I love you" and all that other mushy shit.

* * *

I got off the phone and took a much-needed shower. It was going on seven o'clock by the time I decided to leave the house.

My sisters had really been on my mind, and I thought it would be a good day to visit the cemetery. I asked if White Girl wanted to go, but she declined and went on her own little adventure to visit her family. It was hard to believe I was about to go see my people at a graveyard, but it was a reality I had to deal with. My baby sister Tori would've been nineteen years old next month on her birthday, probably in college pledging a sorority or something like that. She was the light of my life and my reason for breathing; after she was gone, it seemed my light was to dim to see sometimes and that my breaths were shorter and much more strained, making them harder to take. Kierra was the big sister that acted more like the little sister, and she had worked my nerves in every way possible since she got strung out; but all in all, she was still my sister. Sometimes I asked God, "Why them? *Why my sisters?*" I guess I had survivor's guilt, and that shit was slowly killing me.

I parked on the side of the grass at Woodlawn Cemetery and took a deep breath before I stepped from the car. I searched for my sisters' headstones by using the map I got from the secretary and found them in a nice, secluded corner tucked away under a huge weeping willow tree. I got down on my knees and wiped the dirt away from Tori's and then from Kierra's headstones. "Wow. Who would've thought we would all be together again," I said to no one in particular as I took a cross-legged seat under the tree.

I looked at the stones and made a mental note to thank Coco for handling the arrangements for them both. After Tori was killed behind Kierra's bullshit, I paid the cemetery owner for a triple plot because I knew I was going to kill the person responsible for my sister's death or die trying! As for Kierra, I knew that at the rate her ass was going, her life wouldn't last too long either. Little did I know that she would actually die saving me! If the roles were reversed, it would've been me inside the earth had Kierra not showed up.

"Kierra, I know we weren't on the best of terms during the last few months of life, but I swear I never stopped loving you. You chose your own path, and I just had to fall back and let you do you because you weren't ready for my help. That high you was chasing had control over your mind, baby, but I swear not a day went by that I didn't think about you, K." A tear fell from my eye, and I wiped at it quickly. "Tori, I miss you so much, baby sister, and I want you to know that life without you just ain't been the same. You were like my daughter, and I fault myself everyday for not being there to protect you, boo. You were my responsibility, and I fucked up!" Now, the floodgates were open, and the tears just gushed out. "None of us never ever had a chance in life. With our daddy pushing more weight than elephant scales and a cracked-out mother, we weren't expected to be shit! Tori, you could've been somebody—a doctor, a lawyer, or something like that, but now you will never be a mother or a wife. You were supposed to go to prom and like boys, but you died too young—an innocent baby who damn sure didn't deserve the hand you were dealt. I swear on my word that Lucifer is going down if it's the last thing I do." I sobbed until I had no more tears left. I stood and wiped the dirt from my pants and blew a kiss at my sisters, promising that I would return and it won't be so long next time.

Just as I reached for the door handle of my truck, someone called my name. Not knowing who it was, I immediately reached for my gun that was always stashed in my secret hiding spot in the cushion of my passenger seat. I felt around for it as I kept looking behind me; it's never good to turn your back in a situation like that. *Got it!* I thought as I reached for the nine and quickly held it at my side.

"Lovely? Where you been girl?" a male voice asked from the shadows.

I gripped my shit tighter. "Who is that?" I called out, with my heart racing. I squinted a bit because the sunset was hiding his face.

"It's Peanut," he said and walked closer to reveal himself.

Ain't this a bitch! I thought as the nigga who got my sister hooked on drugs walked up to me like we was old homies off the block. "What in the hell are you doing out here?" I rolled my eyes.

"I came to see my girl. It's our anniversary," he said, pointing toward Kierra's plot. I was pissed off! Not only was he there, alive well and talking to me, but he looked hella good for some nigga with AIDS.

"You'll see her all you want soon. Don't your sorry ass got a death sentence?" I knew it was a really fucked-up thing to say to someone, but I didn't care.

"Yo, you ain't right for that!" He shook his head.

"It is what it is, nigga. You got my sister hooked on that junkie shit and gave her AIDS, so I ain't gonna feel bad for you," I spat.

"That's impossible, Lovely. My results were negative."

"What?" I asked for clarification.

"Listen…after all that shit went down with us stealing the dope and Tori being killed over it, I had a reality check. I checked myself into rehab and told Kierra to come with me, but she didn't want to. She said she wasn't ready yet. I stayed in for two months, and when I came out, I found out she'd been turning tricks and prostituting for a taste. She saw me one night a while later and told me she wanted to clean herself up because you needed her—and most of all because she needed you. When she checked into rehab, they tested her and gave her the news. She was diagnosed with full-blown AIDS." When the words came out, he got misty eyed. "She was supposed to get clean and be my wife, Lovely."

"Yeah? Well, what can I do for you?" I asked in a nonchalant tone, thoroughly irritated by the presence of that nigga.

"It's fate that I would run into you today after what I just got wind of, so I guess the question is what I can do for you."

"Okay. So what can you do for me?"

"Look…" He glanced from side to side as if the dead people were eavesdropping. "When I heard you was back, I was hoping I'd run into you, because word in the 'hood is that somebody is tryin' to set you up, ma'...somebody on your own damn team." He pointed to me.

Before I had time to react or respond, I saw the boys in blue rolling up the long dirt road like the hit squad, with lights flashing and all. "Shit!" I looked down at the nine in my hand.

"Put it in the flowers." Peanut nodded to the bouquet of wrapped roses he was extending my way.

Not having another option, I followed his advice just before the cars came close enough to see what had just happened.

"Freeze!" one cop ordered with his gun pointed at us.

I squinted from the bright headlights.

"Get down on the fucking ground!" another cop yelled as he kicked my feet apart, causing me to lose my balance and fall hard. "Lovely Brown, you're coming with me."

"Am I under arrest? Because if I'm not, then I ain't going nowhere," I said, trying to keep my lips away from the ground. My lip gloss was sure to attract the dirt and get all gritty.

"Who the fuck are you?" a black cop asked when he noticed Peanut, who was clutching the roses for dear life.

"I'm her sister's boyfriend—just trying to bring my girl some flowers, sir. That's all." He used the nicety to smooth the cop over.

"Well, go and pay your respects somewhere else unless you want to be tagged into my investigation."

Peanut backed away as the cop cuffed me and yanked me to my feet. I was fucking pissed that my clothes were all dirty; my new Jimmy Choos looked like some Jimmy Whose.

While the cop walked me toward the car, I called back to Peanut, "Who is it?" I eagerly anticipated the answer, but it never came.

The cop yelled back to him, "Keep it moving, or we'll take you in too!"

CHAPTER 20

At the police station, I had been in the interrogation room for about three hours before somebody came inside to talk to me. "Ms. Brown, how are you? I'm Detective Vilan." The young black cop extended his hand.

"I've been better smart ass!" I spat. That son-of-a-bitch knew my hands were cuffed behind my back, so I couldn't shake his.

"Do you know why you are here?" he asked as he sat down across from me.

I rolled my eyes. "No, and I don't give a fuck. Just let me get my phone call."

He sat back in his chair. "What do you want to tell me about your father?"

"I don't want to tell you shit! I'm ready to fucking go. You can't hold me here on no grounds. You know that, right?" I said, smacking my lips.

"Bitch, this is my muthafuckin' house, and at my house, you play by my goddamn rules. I ain't letting your ass go until you start talking about the shit I want to hear." He slammed his hand on the metal table.

I didn't flinch nor move a muscle because I knew he was just trying to get a rise out of me. "Vilan, if you was any kind of real detective, then you would know I ain't spoke to my daddy in five years."

"Bullshit!" he snapped. "The minute your ass turned back up in my city, all hell broke loose. This shit has your father written all over it! His ass is a cop-killer, and so are you!" He stared at me, and I stared right back.

"Look, I don't know shit about no dead cops." I shifted in my seat, trying to get some small comfort from the hard, cold chair.

"So you're telling me you don't know shit about the murders over there on the East Side? Because I have someone that puts you and your friend at the scene." He smirked, thinking he had me, but I knew better.

If that clown had any real shit on me, I would've already been put up under the jail, so I called his bluff. "Okay. Well, if I'm busted and you got me, then we don't need to be in here holding this conversation, right?" Now it was my turn to smirk, but my smile was quickly wiped off when Detective Vilan backhanded me.

"You stupid little bitch! This shit ain't no fuckin' game. I know it was you or your rotten old man. I may not have what I need to lock your ass up and throw away the key right this minute, but I swear on my brother's life that I will hold you here until I get it." He was pouring sweat, and I was tasting blood.

"What the fuck is your problem?" I spit some blood on the floor.

"Your father killed mine in a drug bust gone bad years ago, when my dad was an undercover cop. I ain't never forgot that shit. Now, five years after he escaped from prison, you miraculously turn back up, and my baby brother dies in a similar situation at the hands of the same bloodline."

I opened my mouth to speak, but he raised his hand again and cold-cocked the shit out of me, knocking me and the chair I was sitting in down to the ground. The nigga was going ape-shit, but there was nothing I could do about it; my hands were literally tied—not to mention my gunshot wound from the shootout was still fresh and hurting like a mutha. My eye swelled up in an instant, and I could no longer see. A small tear escaped my free left eye, but not because I was scared or sad. I was angry as hell and couldn't do shit about my situation.

"Bitch, I'm going to kill your ass, even if it wasn't you. I been watching you, and I know your trick ass ain't squeaky clean. Remember the Rump Shaker?" He stomped me in my leg. "Yeah, you nasty bitch. I was there, watching you like a hawk while you stripped and swung on them poles." He stomped again, this time hitting my side.

I screamed out in agony, but no one ever came to rescue me from police brutality; just like the streets, those boys in blue have a code.

"I watched you meet with the Italians on the street in plain sight, like you couldn't be fucked with because you was working for your father. He may have some cops on his payroll, but not this one!" He pointed to his chest like Godzilla, foaming at the mouth and all.

After a few more kicks, I was numb and temporarily pain free, drifting in and out of consciousness. I felt helpless, but at the same time, I understood where he was coming from since it was exactly how I felt when Tori was taken from me. I wanted to kill the person responsible for taking her life, so I did. One night, with the help of White Girl and Do It, I put that fool Spooky, a local drug dealer, out of our misery—only to find out he was the wrong person.

"Detective, is this how you usually conduct your interviews?" some woman asked when she ran into the room, her heels *click-clack*ing on the gaudy tile with every step.

I couldn't see her, but I could hear her. There were a few more people inside the room, but I couldn't see them either. I just lay on the floor in silence. While I was proud that I took my ass-whoopin' like a grown woman, I was happy as hell that the beating was over. I heard more scuffling, like they were trying to wrestle my assailant to the ground, and then the commotion vanished.

I thought I was alone until I heard, "Oh shit, son! She is fucked up." Whoever it was, I knew he was referring to me.

"Yeah. Vilan put a hurtin' on lil mama. You know that's Lucifer's daughter, right?" someone else chimed in.

"No shit! You talking about thee Lavelle Lucifer Brown? The number-one eighties gangsta? This is his daughter in the flesh? No shit! At one point, Lucifer was Detroit's public enemy number one—until he finally caught a case that his ass couldn't beat."

"Yeah, I know. I remember hearing about him on the news so many times growing up. When he went to prison for life, the mayor was on TV…crying and shit and talking 'bout how Detroiters were safe again." The man laughed.

"Hell yeah, I remember that shit. Everybody was happy to get that crazy nigga off the streets. He got a lot of blood on his hands," the other man added.

If I wasn't lying there half-conscious, I would've cussed out both those fools for not checking to see if I was okay. I needed a damn hospital, and those dumb-ass cops was taking trips down Memory Lane.

"No wonder Vilan went psycho on her ass. You know her pops killed his old man, and then last night, he got a tip on his cell phone saying she had something to do with Donald, his little brother, getting killed the other day on the East Side."

As the two continued, and I thought to myself, *tip? What fucking tip?*

"No shit?! Don was the driver of that truck, wasn't he? Damn. I should kick this bitch myself for what she did to those cops."

They abruptly stopped talking, and I heard the familiar heels tapping as the woman entered the room again. I was glad that maybe finally, some help was coming, though I did want them cops to keep talking because the shit had gotten real interesting. They said the driver was an undercover cop, and Meechie told me he had done a bid with him a while back. *What the hell is going on?* I thought to myself.

"Gentlemen, can either of you tell me what the fuck is going on?"

I felt something on my neck, and I assumed it was her fingers, probably checking my pulse. My ass might've been semi-conscious, but I was far from dead and listening to everything they assumed I couldn't hear.

"Well?" She raised her voice an octave or two.

"Um..." they both stuttered, and then one of them finally proceeded, "Last night, Vilan got a tip that she was responsible for the execution of those cops the other day. His brother was one of them, so I guess he took this real personal, boss."

"Okay, but how did he find out where she was, and why in the hell did none of you idiots think to tell me?"

"The same person who gave him the tip about his brother also told him where she was. He followed her when she left the residence and arrested her at the cemetery."

"Shit!" I could tell from the sound of her heels that she was pacing back and forth on the cold, hard floor. "Okay, look...she needs to be checked out by a doctor, but I can't let her leave here until she looks better. One of you fools go and get a medic from down the street. Do you think you can handle that, or is it too complicated for you?"

"Yes, ma'am," one of them said like a scolded child, and I heard someone leave the room.

"You, help me get her down to the individual holding cell in the back. No one can see her like this, or we're gonna be facing a lawsuit out the ass, and this city is already in enough trouble," she said.

I was lifted into the air, and the man who was carrying me asked, "What about when she wakes up?" He was so close I could smell his stale cigarette breath.

"We will just tell her this is what happens when she resists arrest."

Resists arrest? While I'm handcuffed to a damn chair? Well ain't that some shit!

CHAPTER 21

It had been about three days, and I was still stuck in that hellhole they called a holding cell. Those muthafuckas was playing dirty, and I was pissed because it wasn't shit I could do about it. The tiny cell had a small window and wooden bench, I had to ball up if I wanted to get off my feet. They wouldn't let me have the damn phone call they owed me, I'm sure it's because they feared me lawyering up. They hardly fed me, only tossing me a bag of chips and a pop from time to time. Every time I had to pee, I was coincidentally escorted by a male officer who said that by law, he had to stand there and hold the stall door open while I took my pants down to piss. *Give me a break!*

Although I hurt like hell, the person who examined me just said, "It's nothing major—just a few bumps, bruises, a busted lip, and maybe a fractured rib." I wanted somebody to do this shit to him and then tell him to "Walk it off" and "Man up" because it was nothing major!

I couldn't sleep because I couldn't get comfortable, and since I had nothing else to do, my mind constantly raced. I couldn't wait to get out and talk to Meechie's ass about that dead-cop Donald nigga. *Was this nigga lying?* My mind kept telling me the answer was *"No,"* but facts are facts, and that nigga did vouch for him. Hell, if we wouldn't have shot him, that nigga would've been singing like a canary and leading the police straight to us, turning the whole situation way uglier than it already was. Then I thought about White Girl. *Did that bitch go and lose her fuckin' mind and snitch on me?* Again my mind told me *"No,"* because bringing heat on me would've most definitely brought heat on herself since we were both laying our heads down at the same place. But then again, when I asked her to come with me, she declined. *Did she know them boys were coming for me? Did she send them to me?*

I shook my head side to side, trying to get rid of the crazy thoughts. I was starting to lose it. I tried to close me eyes, but they popped back open instantly. "Oh my God!" I thought aloud as images of Shawnie flashed around inside my head. *What if they've been calling my phone and a cop answered? Will they kill my niece—or worse—thinking I ran to the police?* Then another thought came to mind: *What if they don't let me out in time to get her back?* I only had a week left to get the money for Shawnie's ransom, and I wasn't doing shit but wasting time sitting up in this bitch. "Hey, yo!" I called out and then grabbed my side to sooth the pain.

"Shut up!" the cop I had come to know as Sanchez hollered back.

"Man, it's been three days. Can I finally get a phone call?" I limped up to the door to talk through the slim opening.

"Look, I don't make the rules, and you know the lieutenant said no calls, Ms. Brown." The half-Mexican, half-black cop gave me a sympathetic glance. Of all of the assholes I met there, he was the coolest and most respectful of the group. He didn't like what they were doing to me, but it was Detroit. Everybody was crooked, and there was nothing he could do without losing his job.

"Can you take me to the bathroom then?" I didn't really have to go, but I had to get out of that cramped space for a second. Those cells were meant to be temporary. Most people stayed a few hours until the cops couldn't legally hold them any longer, and some stayed overnight to be taken to the courthouse across the street the next day or transported to the next facility on a warrant, but no one ever stayed for three days going on thirty like I was. It was a bit extreme. It was pissing me off and taking me straight to crazy.

"You know the drill, Ms. Brown," he said, expecting me to place my wrists through the hole so I could be cuffed.

"Sanchez, do I look like a threat?"

He knew I wasn't because even though some of the swelling had gone down, I was still lumped up pretty bad, and I doubled over in pain when I walked. Truthfully, I wasn't in any shape to make a jailbreak.

"All right, but please don't try nothing." He looked back behind him to make sure we were alone. He opened the door, and I two-stepped my way down the hall and around the corner to the bathroom with Sanchez in tow.

As I turned to enter the restroom, I heard a very familiar voice. "Well, someone better find her ass right damn now before I have this whole place shut down!" the woman yelled.

I paused to listen.

"Ma'am, I've checked our records twice, and no one by the name of Lovely Brown is here."

"Look…I'm too tired and too old for games. I need her, and I need her now, or I will have the whole goddamn…"

I quit listening and turned to Sanchez, who was already looking at me.

"Ms. Brown, I hope I don't lose my job over this, but now is your chance. You better go for it." He nodded for me to go ahead and walk away, and then he turned his back and walked in the opposite direction.

"Hi. I'm Lieutenant Charles. Can I help you clear up this misunderstanding?"

I tried to move faster, but I couldn't. It was the bitch with the heels, and I couldn't wait to get up in her face. Hurt, battered, bruised, and all, I would use all the strength I had left to cold-cock the shit out of that bitch.

"Lieutenant, I'm Agent Nichols with the FBI, and I happen to know that my suspect is here. I want her now."

I finally made it to the door at the end of the deserted hall, but I had to stop and take a breather before I could go any further because my ribs were killing me. I peeked out the door and saw Agent Nichols and Lieutenant Charles standing face to face. Neither of those bitches were about to back down.

"I don't know who your suspect is. I do apologize, but clearly you've been given some bad information. Let me show you out." The lieutenant tried to turn Agent Nichols to the door, but the older Fed wasn't about to let the younger police woman push her around.

"You have ten minutes to locate my suspect, or your ass will be the one in handcuffs before it's all over," Nichols barked.

Charles didn't miss a beat. "You do what you gotta do, but please believe that when this is over, I will have your job!" When she glanced over at me, she almost gagged on her words.

Nichols turned to see what had caught her off guard, and she had to do a double-take. "Lovely? Is that you? Oh my God!"

CHAPTER 22

I had never been so happy to see alphabets on a Fed's jacket in all my life. She had to cuff me to make the whole suspect story seem authentic. You never know who's lurking around at a police station, and the last thing I needed was the wrong person to see me and the Feds chopping it up like we were homies.

We were in her Navigator and on the freeway in no time. I filled her in on most of what had happened, leaving out the parts about Donald and the shootout, of course. I was beyond funky and sore and in desperate need of a shower, but first I had to get to my truck, which had been impounded. "How did you know where I was?" I asked, looking up from my cell phone, which she made the cops return to me, along with all my other personals that they took. I had just cut it on and it was blowing up like crazy, but there wasn't no way in hell I was gonna answer or make any calls in the presence of a Fed. Hell, I had waited that long, so another thirty minutes wouldn't kill me.

"Well I went to check on Jermaine the other day, and he told me something had to be wrong because you weren't answering your phone. He told me to go over to Coco's salon to see if she had seen you. When I got there, her and Candace were hysterical and basically told me the same thing—that you left the house alone and never returned. I stepped out and began to make some calls.

Just as I got off the phone, getting nowhere, a man came up and went inside the salon. I followed him in, and he pulled Coco to the back to tell her something. As soon as he left the salon, Coco told me he said he was with you when you got arrested…and here we are now, so the rest is history." She lit a Newport, and I cracked my window.

I knew she had to be talking about Peanut, and I made a mental note to meet him and retrieve my gun. "Thanks for the lookout. They was on that bullshit back there," I said, still holding my side; it seemed like we hit every damn pot hole on Woodward Avenue.

"Baby don't take this the wrong way, but I wasn't looking out for you. I was looking out for me. I need your dad before I retire, and you are the only person who can make that happen. I'd been chasing him for years. I finally caught him, put him in jail and thought they threw away the key, only to find out that his ass had a spare set." She laughed. "That's one cold-blooded nigga, but his ass ain't gon' get away this time. I swear on that!"

Me too! I thought to myself. Had I pulled the trigger five years earlier, I wouldn't have been going through this shit. The only good thing to come of the whole experience was the fact that nobody thought I was hard enough to stunt by myself. Everybody thought LB was my dad and that I worked for him. I wasn't complaining at all, because little did she know that Lucifer had taken the heat off of lil ol' me. I wanted to put two in my father's head myself, but I had promised Frankie he would get his money and LB on a silver platter in exchange for my niece so our debt would be settled. But, I had also promised to deliver Lucifer to Nichols in exchange for Maine's freedom. *Decisions, decisions. What's a girl to do?*

* * *

I was pissed when we pulled up to Randy's Pound House and I saw my Porsche torn into pieces and ripped to shreds. My beautiful truck had been demolished. The paint job was scratched immensely, and my smooth peanut butter interior was now more like extra chunky peanut butter with all the damage done to it. My glove compartment door was hanging off; hell, to be honest, my whole dashboard was leaning. My CD player was missing entirely. All my windows were broken, and the custom Starr wheels with the chrome and blue inserts were all bent to hell, probably by a sledgehammer. I would've rather someone stolen them than mangle them like that. "Fuck!" I kicked the driver door closed and then regretted that because it hurt like hell. I walked back up to the Navigator that was parked a few feet away. "As you can see, my shit is fucked up. I need to call for a ride."

"You sure? I can take you wherever you need to go. It's not a problem." She looked over at me and gave a warm smile.

"Let me just sit in the car for a while. I need to think. Is that cool?" I asked.

She nodded like she understood. "Lovely, I'm so sorry." She touched my hand, and that shocked me because it was a polite and affectionate gesture I wasn't used to.

"It's just a truck. I can get something else." I put my head back and closed my eyes.

"Not about the truck, baby. Just about everything," she said, causing me to look up at her.

"What chu mean?" I questioned.

"Honey, what are you? Twenty-five? You are just a baby, but you have been through more things than one person should have to go through in a lifetime. Look at you." She pulled down the visor mirror in front of me, forcing me to take a long, hard look at my beat-up face. "This is what life is doing to you."

"I'm good, though, Mrs. Nichols," I said, feeling comfortable enough to drop the agent title.

"Honey, I've seen 'good' before, and it sho don't look like this." She closed the mirror and folded the visor back up. "If you were my daughter, I would never have you running these streets like a mad woman, getting death threats by everyone and your ass beat by the police, all on account of what your bastard father has done and what your mother didn't do," she said in a calm but loving voice.

Tears slipped down my cheek. "Mrs. Nichols, I tried to be a better person, I swear, but every time I look up, shit is happening, and I gotta fight back. All I know how to do is fight…that and hold everybody around me down." I wiped a tear with my tattered shirt.

"But who is holding *you* down?"

Her question caught me off guard. Normally, I would have been quick to answer, *"Maine, Do it, White Girl, Meechie, and Coco."* At one point, my circle was tight—so tight nothing or no one could infiltrate it—but now Do It was dead and Maine was locked up. Coco had my back to certain degree, like a best friend should, but the shit I was doing and how I was living was way too serious and miles past her skill set. If some shit got poppin' for real, her ass was out by default. Then there were Meechie and White Girl, my hit squad and my people, but until that shit was worked out and I found out who the snitch was, I couldn't trust neither of the two. "You're right. Ain't nobody holding me down. Everybody is out for they self. I didn't want this lifestyle, but it chose me the day that my sister left this world. I ain't got nobody." I cried—and I mean really cried. I had let a few tears fall over the years about this or that, but sitting there while Agent Nichols patted my back, I let it all in sobs. It didn't stop the pain, but it did make me feel better. I hadn't had a motherly woman care for me and give me advice since I was thirteen or fourteen years old, and it really felt good. I knew she was sincere and not just trying to butter me up.

"Lovely, when this is all over baby, promise me you will leave this lifestyle alone. You need to marry that Jermaine fellow because he loves you. Give him some babies and make it your mission to give them all the love and guidance you wished you had growing up so they don't have to learn the things you did. Maybe when it's all over and we aren't on official business—when I'm good and retired—I can come visit you and your children. I don't have any grands, and I so want some."

"You don't have any children?" I asked.

"Just one—my daughter Melanie. She died when she was about your age, caught up in similar shit." She gave me a painfully knowing look. "She ended up taking a bullet meant for her boyfriend, a no-good, lowlife drug dealer who was once the crowned king of Detroit. His name was Raphael, and he had the drug game sewed up because in the eighties, very few people had connections. With crack and heroin on the rise, his connections kept his pockets full. My baby was in medical school and had her whole life ahead of her, but she couldn't shake the love she had for that bastard. I warned like a mother should, but she was grown and not about to hear anything I was saying. He asked her to go with him to make a quick drop to one of his dope houses, she did. Then…" She sighed heavily, letting the pain out before she continued, "Well, that was the last decision my Melanie ever made. Little did either of them know, there was a team of young, cold-blooded killers lurking in the shadows, waiting for Raphael to pull up so they could rob him and claim the throne. As soon as he cut the engine off, the team came out with their guns blazing, lighting up the Camaro like a Christmas tree." She began sobbing, and it was my turn to rub and pat her back.

"Did they ever catch the guy?" I asked, really hoping they did.

"Yes, but it took years, and even when he went to prison, it wasn't for my daughter's murder." She wiped her face.

"Well, he might not have been charged for Melanie's death, but at least he got put away." I was genuinely happy to find out the asshole served time.

"Not long enough, Lovely."

"He got a short sentence?"

"No. He broke out of prison five years ago."

Silence filled the air as the realization of what she was saying hit me like a ton of bricks: Lucifer and his team had killed Agent Nichols's daughter.

CHAPTER 23

It had been an hour since Agent Nichols and I shared our moment in her ride, and now more than ever, I was determined to stop Lucifer and shut his shit down for once and for all. I had her take me to Metro Airport so I could pick up a rental car and get on with my day. After seeing the damage done to my shit, I took all my personal stuff out and kissed my Porsche goodbye for the time being. I had just pulled away from the Hertz rental lot and was on the freeway heading to Coco's house when my cell rung for the thousandth time. "Hello?" I said weakly, cutting down the volume on the radio in the candy apple-red Cadillac CTS.

"What the fuck is up, boo? Where you been?" Maine asked in an aggravated tone, right after I pressed one to accept his call.

Not wanting to send him up in a panic, I calmly said, "Baby, I'm okay, but I was arrested and I—"

Before I could get another word out, he started screaming. "Arrested? What for?"

"Nothing really, I guess. Some cop got a wild hair up his ass for Lucifer, and since he can't get to him, he got his thrills fucking with me." I switched hands because the arm I was holding the phone with was still throbbing from the gunshot.

"They kept you for three muthafucking days, Lovely?" he asked, like shit wasn't adding up.

"Hell yeah. He went ape-shit on my ass, and then I was locked up with no phone calls or nothing. They didn't want nobody to see me all fucked up I guess." Instantly, I regretted the last part, but I'd already spilled it.

"WHAT! He put his hands on you, baby?" he asked, and I could tell he was pissed.

"Yeah, but it's all good. Nichols came through and got me out." I tried to brush it off like it was nothing, knowing damn well I could scream bloody murder at the pain I was experiencing with my every movement. Shit, it even hurt to blink!

"I swear to God, I'm going to see that nigga as soon as I get out," he said, and I knew he was probably pacing the floor with his muscles flexing hard, ready to whoop some ass. That was my nigga, and I knew he would make good on his word, so there was no need for me to downplay it for him or try to change his mind. Maine was already a killer by profession; it was nothing to him to put two in Detective Vilan's thick skull. He'd do it without a second thought and still be home by dinner.

"Okay, boo. Remember who phone you on," was all I said, just to remind him we were being recorded.

"A'ight, ma'. I'ma hit you back later. You swear you good, right?"

"Im a bad bitch, so you know this ain't gone get me down," I said, and we hung up.

* * *

Truth be told, I was a bad bitch, but even bad bitches have bad moments, and I was smack dab in the middle of one of mine. So much shit raced through my mind, and before I knew it, I had arrived back in Detroit. I was so lost in my thoughts that I don't remember anything about the forty-minute ride from the airport: no red lights, no stop signs, and no nothing. That was scary. I pulled up to Lou's Deli to pick up the corned beef sandwich I so desperately wanted because I was starvin' like Marvin, but I was stopped by the sound of my cell phone ringing once again. "Hello?" I answered with attitude.

"Lovely? Girl, are you okay?" White Girl asked.

I smacked my lips. "Hell fuck no, I ain't okay. Look…I ain't got time to be talking on no phone, so meet me around the way in twenty minutes and have everybody there, especially Meechie!" I snapped and hung up. I was so angry I didn't know what to do. On one hand, I wanted to say *"Fuck 'em all"* and leave they snitching asses alone, but on the other hand, I needed them to put an end to the madness. I went inside and got my sandwich, corned beef on rye with Thousand Island dressing and coleslaw, just the way I like it. On my way out the door, I ran right into Peanut.

"My bad, shortie." He looked down, then did a double-take. "Lovely? That you, girl?"

"Yeah, my nigga, it's me. Come over here and let me talk to you for a second." I nodded my head toward my rental, and he hesitated for a second before he reluctantly came my way.

"Them cops did you like that?" He reached to touch my face, but I quickly turned away. "My bad again," he apologized and then did a quick check of the scenery. It seemed like he was still noided about the shit that happened the other night at the cemetery.

"Yeah, you know how it go. But, uh…I just wanted to thank you for taking the piece from me. They woulda sho nuff locked me up if I was caught with that burner." I gave him dapp, and he once again peeped the scene, this time causing me to look too.

"Yeah, no prob', my nigga. Oh yeah…let me get that back to you right quick." He hustled over to his old-school Cutlass, and I followed behind him at a slower pace. When I finally got up to the trunk of his car, he was just lifting the carpet that was on top of the spare tire. As he lifted the tire, he once again did a scan of our surroundings.

"Yo, is there something I should I know?" I feared what his reply might be.

"Naw. I'm just trippin'. Ever since the other night, I feel like

I'm being followed or some shit." He reached for the gun, using a towel he kept in the trunk; I figured he used it when he was fixing his car since it was all dirty and covered in oil, "Let's just make this quick, my nigga."

I took the sandwich out of the paper bag and was about to give him the bag to put the gun in, but I noticed that the nine he was holding wasn't even mine. "Nut, that ain't mines."

"Yes it is. This is the one I got from you that night, when you put it in those flowers." He checked around again and then dropped it like it was hot into the bag.

I looked inside and shook my head. "Nope. Mine's engraved, and this one ain't."

"Lovely, I don't have any guns at all. I'm telling you this is the one I put in my trunk after I left the cemetery. Guns and shit make me nervous. I woulda just tossed that bitch, but I told you I been feeling like somebody is watching me, and I wanted to have a piece on me just in case." He looked around again and again, and I did the same.

"This ain't my gun, Nut." I looked at it one more time to be certain. "But anyway, back to this whole snitching thing…flat out, who the fuck is it?"

He closed the trunk. "I ain't got no names. I'm just hearing that somebody on your team ain't who they say they is, and Lucifer is setting you up for the kill." He glanced around again, but accepting the fact that his ass was just bugging out, I didn't look this time and just kept my eyes focused on him.

"Where you get your info from?"

"Nobody in particular. I just be hearing shit from the fiends at the NA meetings. Half of them come to meetings blazed out they mind, just looking for a place to chill till they come down off that high, and those junkies be talking—rambling on about this or that. I heard your name a few times, and they say it's gonna go down real soon!" He did one last scan. "Just be careful and watch your back, shortie."

The words left his mouth just before somebody on a motorcycle flew through the parking lot like a bat out of hell and put a bullet right between his eyes.

"Oh shit!" I screamed and then dropped to the ground as bullets continued to rip through the air. Not one to go out like that, I reached in my paper bag and retrieved the gun.

POP! POP!

I let off two shots since that was all I had, but they were enough to get me out of Dodge and back to my rental car safely. I peeled out, barely on two wheels, and managed to head in the opposite direction of the shooter. I was home free until I noticed the damn motorcycle had made a U-turn and was coming back my way. "Fuck!" I spat and put the pedal to the metal, weaving in and out of traffic like a professional driver.

BANG! BANG!

I heard the shots, but it wasn't enough to take my attention off the mission at hand. I blew through a red light, causing a Buick to jump the curb. To my luck, that car hit the motorcycle head on. I made a fast turn onto the freeway and broke every speed limit in sight until I got to Coco's house.

CHAPTER 24

The door was open at Coco's place, so I blew inside like a tropical hurricane and slammed the door, causing Coco, White Girl, and Tiny to stare at me in horror and disbelief. "Where is Meechie?" was all I could manage to say while trying to catch my breath.

"He couldn't make it, but he said for you to call him," White Girl answered, looking at me like I was crazy.

"Girl, what happened to you?" Tiny asked with genuine concern as she stood up from the kitchen table. The other two followed suit.

"I'm good," I said, waving them off.

"What the hell is going on, then, and why do you look like that?" Coco chimed in.

I filled them in on the brief details, leaving out Peanut and the role he played in the drama, and then I got right down to business. "Point blank, I was told my circle ain't tight." I made eye contact with them all and continued, "Somebody is running their mouth and trying to set me up. All I want to know is who the fuck it is." I slammed my fist down on the table.

"Running their mouth about what?" Tiny asked, and I remembered she really didn't know enough about me or my dealings to set me up in the first place. All that time, she'd thought LB was my employer; she had no idea that was my alias.

I dismissed Tiny from our meeting, and then I looked at Coco, who had been my bitch since middle school and then at White Girl, whom I had known for about the same amount of time, even though the majority of that time, she was locked up in juvenile. She was also my niece's mom, and I truly doubted she would set me up since I was the only one who could get her daughter back home. I thought about Meechie and how dumb it sounded that he would incriminate himself. If he said I was at the crime scene, that would put him there as well. He was old school, and I know that nigga wouldn't go out like that . After all the shit he'd done, there was no reason to turn into a lowlife snitch. Shit just wasn't adding up the way it should've, and I was more confused than ever.

"Lovely, girl, just calm down. Who told you somebody's trying to set you up?" White Girl quizzed.

"That don't even matter," I snapped.

"I just was thinking that whoever told you this might be the real culprit," she said, trying to defend herself.

"Nope, that's impossible," I snapped as I reached into my pocket for my cell phone to call Meechie.

"Yo?" he answered, as usual.

"Where the fuck is you at?" I spat.

"My bad for missing the meeting, but I had to ride down to Toledo to handle some business. I should be back there tonight though. Everything all right?" he asked.

"I'll see you when you get back!" I said and ended the call.

"L, why don't you go take a shower? I'll get some Chinese food delivered for us, boo. You are super stressed, and I want you to relax." Coco put her hand over mine, which was now trembling.

I couldn't stop thinking about everything that had taken place over the past few days, and more than ever, I just wanted the shit to be done. My mind raced back to the shooter on the motorcycle, and I couldn't help but wonder if he was one of my father's goons or sent by someone else. No doubt I was ready for war, but I wasn't prepared for that shit that killed Peanut. Somebody had caught me slipping, but I vowed that would be the last time. From now on I'd be on my game, and somebody was gonna pay for all the damn shit me and my peoples was dealin' with.

CHAPTER 25

I did as Coco told me to and took a nice, long, hot shower. I would've taken a bath, but I was afraid I wouldn't be able to get out. While I was drying off with a thick blue towel that smelled like lilac fabric softener, I heard a knock at the door.

"Lovely! Boo, the food is here," Coco yelled up to me.

It didn't matter because I was far from hungry, even though I hadn't had a good meal in days and didn't even get a chance to eat my corned beef. The last thing on my mind was any damn sweet and sour chicken. While I was in the shower, I'd made the decision that I had to go post up in a hotel for the next few days until things got worked out and questions got answered. I hated to leave my people, but some alone time was exactly what the doctor ordered.

I came out of the bathroom dressed in a yellow swing dress, a pair of white flip-flops, and my hair pulled back into a damp ponytail. I went into the room and began to put my things into my duffel bag.

"What up?" White Girl asked as she walked into the room carrying a plate of food and a pair of chopsticks.

"Girl, I don't know what's going on around here, and until I get some clarification, I got to bounce and clear my head," I said as I reached for my cell phone charger and unplugged it from the wall.

"L, how you gon' leave in the middle of all of this?" she asked, as if I had no right to come and go as I damn well pleased. "Fuck that dumb shit somebody putting in your ear! Let's stick to the task at hand, which is getting my baby back!"

"Don't you think I know what we need to do?" I said, looking up at her. "Right now I can't do nothing until I clear my head. I'ma get a room somewhere else where I can be by myself and think things through so we can try to get this last little bit of money together for Frankie. Don't worry. I'll be in touch," I said and zipped up my bag.

"Lovely, you ain't in this alone. You need to know that I got your back no matter what. I got more to lose here than anybody, especially if you go down before my baby is back home." She gave me a sincere look, and I nodded my acknowledgment.

I gave her a tight hug and told her, "Look, no matter what, I will hold up my end, but you need to hit the ground running and get all the money you can." I made my way down the stairs and told Coco my plans. She wasn't happy, but she understood, and with that, I was out the door and on my way.

* * *

Just as I was about to ride downtown to the Marriott, my mind led me in the opposite direction, and I found myself riding down my old block. The plan was to sit in the driveway and reminisce about the old days, hoping I might discover a clue in my thoughts about who might be deceiving me, but when I got there, I was distracted by Jessie, the Betty White-looking neighbor.

She waved me to pull over after I blew the horn and waved at her.

"Hey, Mrs. Jessie. Are you okay?" I asked through my rolled-down passenger window as I pulled in front of her house.

At first glance, she winced at the sight of my face but she didn't say anything about it. "Those squatters are back. They are in there right now." She pointed over to my old house and whispered, instantly piquing my curiosity.

"How long have they been in there?" I wanted to know.

"About an hour or so. They should be leaving in a minute, though, because they never stay long." She looked back at her house and jumped when she spotted her husband standing in the door with his arms folded. "I better go before he blows our cover." She winked, and I smiled.

As if on cue, I saw my front door open, and I held my breath for what seemed like hours as someone backed out of the doorway. They appeared to be lifting or pulling something. I leaned in and strained my eyes for a better view, but I finally gave up and sat back in my seat because I couldn't see a damn thing. A few seconds later, I was able to see that the person was a female dressed in some kind of hospital uniform. She was pulling what looked to be a wheelchair. "What the fuck?" I said aloud just as the woman leaned the wheelchair backward and eased it down the three porch stairs. I almost peed myself right then and there when she swung the wheelchair around to face me. There, right in front of my amazed eyes, alive and more well than I thought, was Do It!

CHAPTER 26

I sat in the car at a loss for words as I watched the lady roll my brother down the street. I shook my head in disbelief. My brother wasn't ashes in a vase; he was living and breathing, just a few feet from me. I rubbed my eyes to make sure I wasn't just hallucinating from all the damn stress I was under, but there he was, for real. I pulled off and drove behind them at less than two miles per hour for the three-block radius and quickly pulled into the parking lot of the building they went into. The sign read: "Mueller's Long-Term Rehabilitation Care."

I got out of the car and made my way into the gray building. It resembled a medium-sized house. My knees were shaking like crazy when I opened the door. It chimed to let someone know I was there.

"Just a second!" someone called from the back.

As I stood there, I looked around the living room and took note of the magazines, board games and puzzle boxes scattered over the coffee and side tables.

"I'm sorry for the wait. Can I help you?" said the woman who had just wheeled Do It back there. She had a bright, warm smile.

"Um..." I cleared my throat that had become dry and continued, "My name is Lovely Brown, and I believe my brother is here."

She eyed me with skepticism. "And your brother would be?"

she asked.

"DeShawn Wright," I said.

She put her hand on her hip and mean-mugged me. "Look, I don't know what you are trying to do, but you gotta go now," she said and then tried to show me the door.

I wasn't having that at all. "Listen, boo…I ain't going nowhere without my brother, so—"

"If you don't leave, I will have to call the police," she threatened, cutting me off.

I grimaced at the thought of another run-in with the boys in blue, but I still wasn't about to leave without getting some answers. "You do what you have to do, but I bet you they won't be here before I turn this bitch inside out." I patted my purse.

Her eyes went from my face to my bag, and she knew what I meant and changed her tone. "Look, ma'am…I don't need this. Please just leave," she begged.

"I don't want to tear this place apart, but I will if I have to. For the longest time I thought my brother was dead, but I damn well know I just saw you wheel him in here. I saw him with my own two eyes, and I ain't leaving without him." The tears fell from my eyes, not because I was overjoyed, but because I was getting so angry and about to clock on ol' girl.

"What is your name again?" she asked, as if she was having a light bulb moment.

"Lovely. Lovely Brown." I wiped my eyes.

She walked away and was back in seconds with a picture in her hand. She held it up next to my face, and then she smiled. "Oh my God, it's you!" she said.

I took the picture from her and looked at it. It was a photo of me and Do It at the Roostertail, on my twentieth birthday.

She grabbed my hands and pulled me toward the back of the house, stopping at a closed door. "DeShawn was shot nine times and left for dead on the side of the road. Three of the bullets did the most harm, and the first one is still lodged in his head, causing severe headaches and short-term memory loss. The second bullet hit his spine, resulting in immobility on his left side, and the third bullet earned him a colostomy bag." I supposed she was just updating me so I wouldn't be so shocked when I saw him.

"How long has he been here?" was all I could say.

"He has been here ever since he was released from the hospital, about eight months after the shooting. That was why I wanted you to leave. He told me that if anybody ever came looking for him, I should call the police since they were probably coming to finish the job." She gave an apologetic look and then proceeded to open the door.

I stopped her. "How did you figure out I was telling you the truth?" I asked.

She held up the picture. "He has a board of good people and bad people. Needless to say, you were on the good side," she answered and opened the door.

I took a deep breath and then followed her in.

"DeShawn you awake?" she asked in a calm voice and then turned to me. "Sometimes he dozes right off after our stroll through the neighborhood. Just like a baby, the fresh air makes him sleepy."

"Lisa, who did you bring?" I heard Do It say, and my eyes watered.

"It's a surprise." she said, blocking his view of me.

"I don't like surprises," he said in a flat tone

I took that as my cue to show my face. "You never did, big bro." I ran up to his bed and wrapped my arms around him, and he flinched. When I backed up, I noticed that he was shirtless, exposing his colostomy bag, and I apologized immediately.

"Lo? Is that you?" He stared at my face.

I just shook my head because my voice was caught in my throat.

He stared a few more moments, and then a tear slid down his cheek, causing me to cry harder.

"I thought you were dead, man. I missed you so much." I reached for some tissue near his bed and blew my nose.

"Man Lo, I missed you and Candace more than you will ever know. I thought you was long gone." He wiped his face and I smiled; he was still keeping it as gangster as always.

"Oh my God! Speaking of White Girl, I have to call her." I reached for my cell phone, but before I could dial, Do It shook his head at me. "What's wrong?" I asked.

"Don't tell her I'm here. I don't want her to know. She can't see me like this."

"Do It, she don't care how you look. You know that. She has been without you for five years," I said.

"No! Lo there are some things that should be left alone. I ain't the man she used to love. I'm a muthafuckin' handicap!" he snapped.

I can't say I didn't understand, but I thought that he was being unfair. Still, I had to follow his wishes. "Okay. On my word, I won't say anything, but—"

He cut me off. "But nothing. You bet not say nothing." He looked at me sternly.

I looked around the room, trying to be funny and change the mood.

"So, what's new? Why are you here? How did you know I was here, and how long have you known?" he rambled on.

"Ain't nothing new. I just found out you was here when I saw you coming out of the old house. I'm here on some unfinished business with you-know-who." I pointed at a newspaper clipping of Lucifer that was pinned on the bad side of the board hanging across from his bed.

"What happened?" he asked.

I gave him the sugar-coated version, not mentioning Shawnie or anything that might upset him. After I gave my spill, I turned the tables on him, because I needed some answers, and I'd waited long enough. I didn't want to start right out with the serious questions, so I danced around them. "Why were you at the old house?"

"They say my mind ain't working the same no more and I be forgetting shit, so every since I came here, we do brain exercises that jog my memory. One day a few years ago, Lisa..." He nodded his head over to the girl who had let me in; I had totally forgotten she was still there, but she was standing by the wall, listening intently. "Lisa took me outside to stroll the neighborhood to see if any of the street names were recognizable. They weren't, but when we stopped in front of the old house, I remembered that I used to live there. I told Lisa we kept a spare key in the backyard under the stone flowerpot. We looked though the glass and saw that it was kind of messy, like nobody lived there anymore, so we went in and looked around. I found a few items and some old pictures, and my memory sort of came back. I've been making progress, so we been going there once a month. It ain't nothing new there to find, but sometimes, Lo, if I just sit in the space, I feel like I'm closer to finding out what happened to me. I cut newspaper stories out about people I know to see if I remember anything about what happened to me. I saw a few stories about your pops and a story about Kierra," he said.

Finally, it all made sense about what I'd seen in the house when I went there to get our stash that day. Do It was the one who'd left all the newspapers and pictures scattered around. "Wow! That's deep!" I said and then moved on to the next question. "When you did you start to remember? How come you never looked for us to tell us you survived?"

"Because I ain't the same. Look at me," he demanded with pain in his face.

"Do It, you know none of this shit matters to us. We are family, and no matter what, you know we got your back," I snapped, because his ass was being selfish.

"I know that, Lo, but right now I ain't no good to nobody—especially not White Girl and my daughter." His gaze caught mine.

"You remember that White Girl was pregnant?" I asked.

He nodded his head and weakly raised his right hand to point over at his nightstand. There was a stack of photos lying there, and I picked them up. The first one was an ultrasound picture, and the second was a picture of Do It kissing White Girl's belly. Then, there was one of White Girl's pink baby shower invitations. I put the stack down.

"What's her name?" he asked as tears rolled down his cheek.

"DeShawna Tori Wright," I said proudly, and I knew her name would make him smile. "We mostly call her Shawnie."

"DeShawna, huh?" He grinned. "She is about five now, right?" he asked.

I nodded.

"Do she look like me?"

I pulled my cell phone out of my purse and showed him a picture Shawnie had taken just a couple days before those bastards snatched her off the bus. She was posing for the camera like a true diva, and I'd made it my screensaver.

"Damn! My baby is gorgeous. Do she know about me?" he wondered.

"Of course."

He was silent.

"You know I wouldn't have it any other way, brother." I patted his back.

"Thank you," he said as he stared at the phone.

"For what?" I asked.

"For keeping your word and getting them out of Detroit safe." He blinked back a few tears.

"Man, you know my pedigree. I always keep my word," I assured him, trying to make light of the situation.

"Is she still safe?" He looked up at me with eyes that wanted the truth.

I lied because I had to. "Yeah, it's all good, bro."

"Good. I wouldn't expect anything less of you and her mother. I wish I could've kept us all safe." He stared off, and I new he was thinking about the past. "Lo, I get so upset with myself when I think about what I let happen to me. If I would've been on my game, shit would've been different, but I guess it don't matter now. Whoever did this to me is probably long gone by now." He looked over at me.

"So you can't remember anything about that night?" I said, finally asking the question I'd wanted to ask since I walked into the room.

"All I remember is sitting in the whip waiting for you. Somebody in a mask put a gun to my head and told me to hop out or they would blow my brains out right then and there. He sounded really familiar, but I did as I was told because that ain't the kind of threat a nigga should take lightly. When I stepped out of the truck, I was hit with something, and I woke up in a dark, wooded area. He called you and told me to say my last words, and then he told me to get down on my knees and beg for my life," he said.

"When I die, it's gon' be on both feet. Never knees in the dirt!" I added. I remembered hearing Do It say that very same thing before two shots rung out and my signal faded, dropping the call.

"He stood there for about ten minutes to see if I was dead, and I did my best not to move or even breathe," Do It said before he went into some type of shock. His body was twitching and jerking, and it scared me straight up out of my seat.

The lady I had come to know as Lisa went right into action. "Please step out for a minute," she said calmly in a polite bitch-move kind of way.

CHAPTER 27

As I sat in the living room of the rehabilitation center, I prayed that my brother would be okay. I didn't want to lose him again, for real this time.

Another lady in scrubs came inside, holding the hand of an older white man, who was crippled up, drooling, and wearing a helmet. "But I don't wanna come inside!" he protested.

"John, we have been outside for two hours in the backyard planting in our garden. Don't you think we need some rest?" she said like a mother, even though the man was probably two times her age.

"Don't like rest," he whined.

"John, what about me? I like rest." She looked at me and smiled. "Oh, hello. Can I help you?"

"No, ma'am. Lisa already helped me." I smiled back and pointed down the hall.

"Okay," she said and then went back to helping John take his helmet off. Then she wiped his mouth of drool and led him upstairs.

"I'm sorry about that, Lovely, but he gets like that when he thinks about the shooting. It's like a panic attack, but because his mobility is off, his nerves just go every which way," said Lisa as she sat down beside me.

"No need to apologize. I'm just glad that you were there and knew what to do," I said honestly. "Hey, Lisa, how did he make it to the hospital?" I wondered.

"From what I was told by hospital staff, he crawled up to the side of the road and was spotted by some paramedics, of all people, who were parked there taking their lunch break," she said. "Turned out to be a lucky break for him!"

"Wow. And I guess the rest is history, huh?" I said.

She nodded. "Lovely, I hate to be rude, but do you think you could stop by tomorrow? After those attacks, he gets so worked up that I have to give him a sedative to calm him down. He'll be out like a light for a good long while now," she said.

"Sure. Tell him I love him and that I'll definitely be back." I stood to leave and then turned around. "Thank you, Lisa, for taking care of him. I can tell you really care for him."

"Yes, DeShawn is my favorite patient," she whispered. "My grandmother opened this place years ago because she loved to help people with disadvantages. When I was a little girl, I watched her, and it became my calling too," she said with pride.

I thanked her again and was out the door in minutes.

The minute I hit the fresh air, I wanted to jump for joy and scream to the world that my brother was alive, but I kept my composure, got into the car, and then shouted a loud "THANK YOU!" to Jesus. I so badly wanted to call White Girl, but a promise was a promise, so I started the car and went to find a hotel nearby.

I was in luck because I spotted a Courtyard Marriott about ten minutes down the road. I grabbed my bag and locked the car, then headed up to the check-in counter just as my cell phone rang. *Damn! I hate when that happens*, I thought to myself. I couldn't answer my phone that minute because it would have been rude while I was checking in, and I couldn't reach it to look at the caller ID anyway. I exchanged pleasantries with the man behind the counter, paid for the room for five nights, got my room keycard, and headed to the elevator. Just as it arrived and I was preparing to get on, a man and a lady walked up behind me to get on as well. I couldn't see their faces, but I could see a distorted image through the reflection of the gold elevator doors.

"Baby, can you believe it's our first wedding anniversary?" She popped her chewing gum. "And yo' mama thought we wouldn't make it because you are too educated for my ghetto ass." She cracked up laughing.

I pressed the button for the third floor.

"Yeah, I wish I could've taken you on a real trip, but with everything going on at work and then my brother getting killed, that kinda put a damper on my plans," he said.

I had to turn slightly to see if he was the asshole I thought he was. The minute we made eye contact, I recognized Vilan, and he recognized me right back. I made sure he knew who I was because I removed my sunglasses to show his ass what the hell he'd done to me. "What's your name?" I asked his annoying giggly wife.

"Desiree," she said. "Why?"

"Desiree from West Seven Mile, right?" I asked, and Vilan grimaced at me.

"Naw, girl. I'm from East Seven Mile, right off Conant," her dumb ass said, letting out a laugh.

"Oh, my bad, girl. You look just like an old friend of mine."

Ding!

Once the elevator reached my floor, I smiled. "Well, even though I don't know you, Desiree from East Seven Mile right off Conant, enjoy your first anniversary, girl." I smiled at Vilan, daring him to try me again. He knew I'd be right there in his girl's neighborhood, going door to door with my shotgun if I had to in order to fuck up his shit real good.

As soon as I was inside my room, I put my bag on the desk, reached inside my purse for my cell phone, and saw that I had missed calls from Maine and Coco. Knowing that I couldn't call Maine back, I had to settle for Coco.

"Hey, girl! You all right?" was the first thing she said.

"Yeah, I'm good. What are y'all doing?" I slipped my shoes off.

"I'm at my boo's house, and White Girl left after you did, but I didn't ask her where she was goin'," she said.

"Okay. Well, I just wanted you to know I'm posted, and I'll probably be by there in a day or two to get that money."

After I hung up, I closed my eyes and got comfortable on the bed. The queen wasn't exactly my Cali King from back home in Ann Arbor, but it sure beat the hell out that jail bench.

"Okay. Have you heard from old boy yet?"

I knew she meant my dad, and to my surprise, his ass hadn't made a peep. If I knew him, though—which I did, he would definitely show his sorry face at the party. "Nope, but I ain't worried. He will be there," I said and then yawned.

"All right, L. Get some sleep," she said and hung up.

I was out for all of thirty seconds when my phone rang again. I didn't look at the caller ID, figuring she'd just forgotten something and was calling me back. "Hello?"

"I knew you couldn't stay away. Detroit is your blood, baby," the caller said.

I bolted straight up in the bed. It was a voice I recognized and never wanted to hear again.

CHAPTER 28

"Long time, no hear from," I said to Lucifer in a cold tone to match his, even though I was nervous as hell.

"Yeah, well, I've been busy since the last time I saw you, but I heard you were looking for me and thought I'd take a break from business to see what my little girl could possibly want from Daddy," he said, cool as a cucumber.

"I wanted to see if we could partner up and have the best of both worlds. You and me could really do some damage," I lied, going right into my Oscar-worthy performance of the bullshit speech I'd prepared for this very moment.

"I don't know if you heard, baby girl, but I'm from the old school. I do my dirt by my lonesome," he said.

"Yeah, that's understandable, but I'm from the new school, and networking gets you everywhere," I shot back. "Shit, two heads is better than one. With me and you on the same team, Daddy, we can make history. I ain't never heard of a father-daughter team runnin' the shit we'd be runnin'." I relaxed back onto the bed, feeling that my words were getting through. I had planned that conversation out the night Maine was locked up. I had strategically come up with a bomb-ass plan to satisfy everybody. First, I'd put the party together and invite the FBI, dressed as regular partygoers, of course. Lucifer would indeed show up with his curious, vengeful ass, and I would hand him over without a care in the world. After they took him into custody, I'd follow behind the FBI car to get shit poppin'. On the flipside, I would have Frankie's people set up a detour or road block so the FBI would have to take an alternative route that would lead right up to Frankie himself. They would put a bullet in Lucifer's head and the FBI agent—unfortunate but necessary. Finally, I would get my niece back. It would be easy enough to stage the whole thing to look like Lucifer got out of the handcuffs and shot the agent, then fled the scene, never to be seen or heard from again since his body would be long gone. After that, Nichols would have no choice but to return Maine, and all would be well with the world again.

"You still got your connect with the Italians?" he asked.

I smiled. He was like putty in my damn hand. "Yep."

"And you want to do all of this even after what I did?" he asked, understandably skeptical.

"Hey, like you taught me, what's done is done. Ain't nothing I can do about it now. It's been five years, and I'm ready to get back to work," I said with ease.

"All right. Let's meet and talk this over," he suggested.

"I'm having a welcome back party Friday. Stop by, and we can put aside our beef over a few Long Islands."

"I'm more of a Cognac man, and I don't do public places like that," he answered.

"Look, if we gon' do this thang, you gotta meet me halfway. I would feel safer in a public place, because I doubt you'll try to kill me in a room full of people. I can have you brought in through the back door and escorted up to the VIP lounge. Me and you will talk privately there, but it's a glass room, so everybody on the floor can see up there and call the police if shit gets funny," I said.

He laughed. "It's a date then," he said.

"Don't you need the name of the place?" I asked.

"No. I've heard the radio announcement more times than I can count," he said and hung up.

I was too geeked that my plan was actually official. *Things are going to be okay after all*—or at least I hoped so.

CHAPTER 29

My day was off to a good start. I had eaten breakfast downstairs in the lobby and came back up to take a shower. I was dressed in a red Ed Hardy one-piece that showed every curve, white wedge sandals, white JLo hat, and of course my stunner shades, since my face still wasn't back to normal. I grabbed my purse and was out and about in no time. The plan was to hit up a few old baller friends of mine. Some were little league and some were major league. Regardless, I had to come up with a little over $450,000, so a baller was a baller in my book.

I got in my car and got ready to call Coco because I knew she still had numbers for most of the people that we used to dance for. I needed to reach out to them, but to my surprise, she called me first. "I was just about to call you, girl," I said as I started the car.

"Straight up. I guess great minds do think alike. Well, let me tell you why I called. I want you to meet De'Andre today for lunch, and I ain't taking 'no' for an answer," she said just as I was about to tell her I was too busy.

"Coco, boo, I'm out here trying to get the rest of this money for Shawnie. Can lunch wait until tomorrow?" I asked as my line clicked.

"Hey, this is White Girl on the other line. Let me hit you right back," I said.

"You ain't got to hit me back. Just meet me at The Purple Room at five…and you better not be late," she said and hung up.

I clicked over. "Hey! Wassup?"

"Hey, girl. Where you at?" she asked.

"On my way to try to find some money," I said and put my car in drive, not even knowing where I would end up.

"That's what I'm calling you for. I just came up on twenty," she said excitedly.

"Oh yeah? From where?" I asked.

"Somebody that owed me a favor from back in the day."

"Okay, so that's w'sup?" I said.

"Yep. Just two more days, and my baby will be home, L. I know we gon' get the rest of this money."

I could tell she was smiling, and so was I.

"Oh yeah…you know what?"

"What?" I asked.

"I been thinking about this whole setup thing, and I'm telling you that Meechie's name is ringing out loud and clear to me. Think about it, L. Who else could it be? Whoever gave you your information said it was somebody close to you, right?" she asked.

"Right," I answered.

"Well, look at the damn facts. Who is close to you? Maine is locked up, and you know that fo' sho. Coco and Tiny asses don't know nothing about nothing, and you know that fo' sho. My daughter is missing, and everything we are doing is to get her back, and you know that fo' sho. What do we know about Meechie?" She paused then continued, his ass been here in Detroit for five years without us, and a lot can change in five years. For all we know, that nigga could be working for your dad again. Real talk, that nigga has been real convenient and accommodating lately—too easy if you ask me. I say we call that nigga up, get the money, and kill his rat ass," she said, all hyped.

Although I was silent, I took heed to everything she was saying, and I had to admit she was making a lot of sense.

"You hear me, L? I'm telling you that nigga ain't to be trusted!"

"Yeah, dog, I hear you," I said as my mind overloaded with thoughts.

"Okay, but are you *listening*?" she said.

"Yeah, I'm listening. Just thinking, that's all. Uh, let me hit you back. I'm going to call Meechie and make some shit right. I'll call you back later," I said and closed my phone, tossing it on the passenger seat. *Damn. What am I going to do now?* I felt like White Girl was right, and I did need to cut ties with Meechie, but my head was in the lion's mouth, and I had to think of a very creative way to pull it out with ease. He had the majority of the money, and getting him to hand it over wasn't going to be easy. At times like this, I really needed some neutral person to talk to, somebody who could give me good advice. Without hesitation I made my way back over to Do It.

Lisa was sitting on the huge porch enjoying the sunshine with him when I got there. "What up, doe?" I said in our usual Detroit greeting, and they both responded the same.

"Lo! What's good, ma'? You look like something got you vexed." He looked at me as I walked across the porch to take a seat in one of the wicker seat next to Lisa.

"Yeah, something like that." I nodded.

"You want to talk about it?" He gave me a concerned look.

"Well, to make a long story short, somebody is holding something very important for me, and lately something ain't adding up with them. It's like they on some other shit but still pretending to be cool and smile in my face like everything is velvet. I need to cut ties with them ASAP, but I don't know how to do that and get what they been holding for me at the same time." I spoke in codes because Lisa was still on the porch. She was a very nice person, but in Detroit, you never know who people knew or are affiliated with, so I never took nothing for granted when talking in the company of others outside my circle, and I didn't want to ask her to leave because that would have seemed rude.

Do It rubbed his chin then, with his good hand, he removed his brown Detroit baseball hat and scratched his head, causing his long dreads to shake.

"Wow. You have dreadlocks," I said and then stared at him. I didn't know how I missed them before, but they looked really good on him. They were neat, and his facial line-up was crispy. It was definitely a good look for him. As a matter of fact, Do It's whole attire was crispy. He had on a pair of brown signature Gucci loafers, white denim shorts, the matching signature Gucci belt, a white wife-beater with a white Polo shirt draped across his shoulder, and of course his gold wood-frame Cartier glasses.

"Yeah, Lisa been locking my hair since I got here, and she takes me to the barbershop once a week. You know a nigga gotta stay fresh, even though I'm fucked up." He laughed, but I just rolled my eyes.

"You ain't fucked up, so please stop saying that!" I shouted.

"Anyway, back to your problem. I think you gotta meet this person and just tell them like it is. If they willing give you what you need without no bullshit, then they ain't got nothing to hide, but if they try to play you out and give you some bullshit, then you know you were right about them." He put his hat back on and then turned to look at the door that had just opened, giving me a glimpse of the huge diamond in his ear.

It was John and the lady from yesterday. "I don't want to plant in the garden," he whined.

"John, you love to plant in the garden, remember?" she said and helped him to the stairs, looking at us and shaking her head.

"No, Carrie. I like naps," John said.

I had to laugh a little, because just yesterday, he was whining about going inside to take one.

They made their way down the stairs and around back.

"Okay, so if I am right about this person and they give me

problems about getting what they holding for me, how do I get it back?" I wondered aloud.

Do It just looked at me. "And they say *my* memory is bad." He laughed. "Lo, you was there back in the day, right? You know how we used to get down," he said and looked at me like I had lost it.

I knew what he was saying, so I didn't say anything I just nodded. I was about to get up to leave and go do what I had to do when my cell phone rang. "Hello?"

"If I had to call your ass one more day and you didn't answer, this little black girl would've been toast," the voice said in a malicious tone that sent chills up my spine, immediately jolting me straight up in my seat.

"Sorry about that. I ran into a few snags, but I'm good now. Is my niece all right?" I stood and walked across to the other side of the porch, trying my best to whisper.

"Yeah, she's good for now. Is Frankie's money all right?" he asked in a dry tone.

"Yep, safe and sound right here with me," I lied.

"You've done good, Paradise. What about Lucifer? If you have him, we can meet tonight," he answered.

"No, I don't have him yet, but I will on Friday. Call me back tomorrow so I can give you the rundown on the specifics," I said.

"All right. You got it," was his reply.

"Can you put her on the phone?" I stepped down off the porch and waited for my baby to come to the phone.

"Auntie L, I'm ready to come home." She sounded so sad, and it broke my heart.

"Auntie is going to get you home, baby. Just hold on until Friday. Do you know how long away that is?"

"No," she said.

"It's only two days, baby. Are you hurt? Have you eaten?" I asked, my heart breaking with every question.

"No, I'm not hurt, and I just ate a peanut butter and jelly sandwich. Auntie L, I thought you and Uncle Maine told me bad people could not get us?" She was crying, and I began to do the same. "I miss you and my mommy. I'm ready to come home. I don't want to wait until Friday."

"Shawnie, I swear on my life that I will get you home, baby. I promise." My tears silently slipped down my face, and I brushed them away. I could only imagine what her five-year-old mind was thinking. I knew she was miserable, and it made me sick to my stomach.

"We will be in touch tomorrow," the man said and then ended the call.

I took a deep breath and wiped my face before I turned around because I knew Do It would pick up on my emotions real quick.

"Yo, Lo," he called from behind me.

I almost leapt out of my skin. "Huh?" I turned to see him at the stairs with concern on his face.

"Let's go for a walk," he said and made his way down the handicap ramp.

* * *

We headed down the block, leaving Lisa on the porch reading a magazine.

"What's up?" I tried to sound casual.

"I heard parts of your conversation, and I feel like you ain't telling me everything," he said, pressing the switch to make his wheelchair go forward.

"Naw, I'm good. Everything will be fine," I said, looking down at the ground, kicking at a rock that was in my path.

"Lo, you know you are my best friend, my sister, my partner, and I know when you lying. Just be straight up. If you are in trouble, let me know."

We stopped at the end of the corner and let a car pass before we crossed the side street.

"Well, I have been telling only half the story, but that's cuz I don't want you to get upset. I feel like knowing too much shit ain't good for you right now," I said.

"Not knowing ain't good either, Lo, because then I'll just worry about it. So what's good? I heard you say 'Shawnie'. That's my daughter, so I think I deserve to know," he said, and he was right.

"Okay, I see your point. Well about two weeks ago, Shawnie was kidnapped. I put her on the school bus, but she never made it to school. When we got home after going up to her school, there was a box on the porch with a note in it from Frankie. He pretty much said he took Shawnie because of what happened to his nephew, and—"

"What happened to his nephew?" Do It asked.

I remembered he didn't know because he wasn't in the truck when I came back. "Remember when you took me to the pizza parlor to pick up the last package from Frankie's nephew so we could flip the business over to Meechie?"

He nodded.

I continued, "Well, when I got inside, I waited and waited in the front, but nobody ever came, so I went to the back. There was dead lady on the floor, two headless men in the freezer, and in the back office, there was a young boy with his neck slashed and his penis stuffed in his mouth. I removed it, and he told me LB had did it all. He said LB also took the money from the safe and the coke I was supposed to pick up. Somebody had also wrote 'LB' on the wall in blood." I caught my breath.

"Damn." Do It shook his head.

"So, back to the present, I called the number Frankie wrote in his note. His guy told me Frankie wants six million dollars and LB by this Friday. Maine went to get the money, but the Feds had closed his accounts, and they took him to jail. I put together some of the old team, and we hit a few licks to get the money up. I'm about $450,000 short, and I think I have Lucifer in the bag, but now I have to also get the rest of the money from Meechie. He has helped me and White Girl a lot, for which I'm thankful, but the other day, I ran into Peanut, and he said he heard through the streets that somebody on my team is shady and is trying to set me up. Right after that, I had a run-in with the cops and had my ass beat like a Hebrew slave. White Girl think Meechie is the rat, and I might have to agree with her, but he got the money that I need to get Shawnie back."

After I finished shedding light on all the details, we stopped at a park. I walked up to the wooden bench and took a seat with Do It parked right beside me.

"Just tell that nigga the money is due on Friday and you want to get it tonight or tomorrow morning just so your mind can rest knowing it's in your possession. Then, once you have the money and the deal is sealed with Frankie, go back to Meechie and confront him about the allegations," he said.

"That's real talk. Well, at least that's one problem solved." I laughed. "Shit, I still got to get the other part of the money and then hope Lucifer's ass shows up." I rubbed my temples and checked my phone again.

"Lo, is my little girl okay?" he said, scratching his beard.

"Yeah, she is good. They let me talk to her just now, and she said they've been feeding her and she hasn't been hurt. Shawnie is a strong little girl like her daddy. Believe that," I reassured him.

"I always prayed she would be." He looked at me. "Lo, I swear that not one day has gone by that I didn't think about her. I knew you would keep your promise and get her to safety, so I didn't worry about that, but I've wondered how she looks, what her voice sounds like, what her first word was, and things like that. I just wish I could turn back the hands of time and get out of the game before this crippling shit happened to me. They say one day I could possibly regain mobility in my left side and I might be able to walk again, but I ain't sure I believe all that."

"Do It, you have got to stay strong. Don't let this get you down. This, too, shall pass. The main thing is that you're alive! I can't tell you how much hurt and pain we went through thinking you were dead. Poor White Girl is still going through it because she don't know w'sup." I shook my head at him.

"Man, I know what you saying, but the man she used to love is gone, L."

"He's not gone, big brother—just different. At least give her a chance to fall in love with the new man you've become. If somebody loves you, they love you no matter what, flaws and all," I said.

"Yeah, I feel that, but part of me don't even want to give her that chance because she might just walk away. I couldn't handle that," he said honestly.

I felt for him, but I still didn't think he was being fair. I felt like I was being put in the middle because from that point forward, anytime I heard her mention him, I'd have to play along with this foolishness. Matter of fact, I couldn't believe the fool had me wasting tears and going to funeral homes for his ass when he'd been breathing the whole damn time. The more I thought about it, the more confused I got. *If he was alive this whole time, why in the hell did somebody take the time to plan and pay for the fake funeral?* "Do It, did you know somebody threw you a funeral?" I asked, though I was sure he didn't have anything to do with that. To my understanding, it happened seven days after he was shot, and he wasn't in any position to go through the motions while he was still in the hospital.

"Naw, I ain't know I had a funeral. Damn." He laughed. "I just thought the 'hood would write a nigga off and charge it to the game. That was why I just stayed out here, changed my look, and laid low." He looked at his watch.

"Now that's another thing I gotta add to my list," I said and stood.

"Why you say that?" He looked at me in confusion.

"Because whoever took the time to give yo' alive ass a funeral is probably the same person who put you in this predicament, if you get my drift." I formed my hand in the shape of a gun and made a shooting gesture.

His face turned stone solid while he thought about what I had said. "Ain't that a bitch? You probably right, Lo." He got pissed, and I worried he might have another attack without Lisa around. "You gotta find that muthafucka and let me put nine bullets in his ass and see how he like it."

"I got you fo' sho!" I said before we made our way back to the center.

Just as we got in front of the driveway, Lisa came out of the house. "I was just on my way to find you. It's time for your meds," she said.

"Look, bro, I'm out. As you know, I got a lot on my plate." I bent down and gave him a soft hug.

"Come and see me tomorrow. I have something for you," he said in my ear, and I nodded that I would.

CHAPTER 30

As soon as I pulled off, I pulled out my phone and called Meechie.

"Yo," he answered, calmly as always.

"What the fuck happened yesterday?" I questioned since he never hit me back when he got back from Toledo.

"My bad, L. Shit got away from me. What's up wit' chu?"

"What's your twenty?" I asked, trying to find out where he was.

"I'm at my crib on Snowden," he answered.

"All right. I will be there in fifteen minutes, my nigga," I said and ended the call without giving him an opportunity to protest.

I pulled up to the old, white, two-story house and parked in the driveway. I walked up to the side door and tapped twice. I waited about a minute before the door swung open right before I raised my hand to knock again but the door swung open.

"What up, doe?" he said in a tone I couldn't really read; I didn't know if he was upset I was there or if he was just coming off a buzz.

"What's good? Can I come in?" I looked at him, standing there in a gray pair of basketball shorts, white ankle socks, and a gray And1 T-shirt.

"Fo' sho, my nigga." He moved aside, and I followed him into the bare kitchen.

There were the usual appliances—a stove and fridge—but nothing else: no dishes, no table, no microwave, nothing. I knew he had two homes, and I guessed this one was not the one where he laid his head.

"Look…my bad about yesterday, but—"

I cut him off. "Uh, it's nothing. Don't worry about it." I wanted to make it seem like everything was okay. "The reason I stopped by is to pick up that money. The deal goes down in two days, and I need to make sure I got it all with me. I don't need nothing to happen between now and then without that money in my hands," I said as best I could without giving away my true feelings. I stared at his unchanged expression for a second, and to my surprise, he smiled.

"Yeah, no doubt! Two more days, and lil shortie will be home. That's wassup! Help me get this shit into your car." He went to the fridge and opened it to reveal stacks and stacks of money, and there was even more in the freezer. "You sure you got a safe place for this?" he asked.

I nodded.

It took us almost two hours to load up the car, and Meechie didn't show any signs of being upset or angry. Though I was glad it didn't get ugly, I was bewildered to say the least..

"All right, L. Hit me up and give me the rundown for Friday. I know you're going to need some backup." He closed the trunk and turned to face me.

"You know what, Meechie? You've been very helpful, but I think I'ma need you to fall back on this one. Me and White Girl got it covered from this point forward," I said. Now that I had the money back, I didn't give a fuck—especially if he was a snitch ass, setting me up.

"What?" He looked at me like he had heard wrong.

"Look, the other day somebody told me my circle ain't tight and that somebody in my crew is trying to set me up. Only two people know in detail what I'm into, and one of them has everything to lose if I go down," I said, reaching inside my purse.

"Oh, so you think it's me? The muthafucka that hit the streets for your ass when you needed help? The muthafucka that just handed you millions of fuckin' dollars without asking for a dime? Fuck you and that light-skinned bitch!" he spat.

"Meechie, I'm sorry you feel like that. I appreciate the help, and like I said, as soon as Maine get out, I'ma break you off, no doubt. But right now, I gotta look out for me. I been thinking over this day and night since the police locked my ass up, telling me they have a witness putting me at the scene of that shit over on the East Side. To be honest, it's not looking good for you," I said. I hated to lose a friend, especially when I had no concrete evidence, but my back was against the wall.

"You got locked up and they said they have a witness?" He smacked his lips. "That shit is crazy, because they took me down for questioning two days ago and pulled the same thing. Obviously they don't got no witness, because we are both standing here looking at each other." He rubbed his goatee.

"Wait a minute…you got taken in too?" I asked.

"Yeah. Some detective fishing for information held me for 'bout two hours and I was out. I tried to call you, but you ain't answer," he said as he reached into his pocket for a Black & Mild. "Did they say something to your girl?" he asked.

"No."

He shook his head at me. "I'm out of it, and you do what you want, but if only three of us know what happened and were the only witnesses, how come only two of us got taken in?" He puffed his slim cigar and looked me square in the eye.

I didn't know what to say, so I told him I would find out and let him know.

"L, you ain't got to let me know shit. You the only one around here that don't know the answer." He turned to go back into the house, but I called out his name. "Yeah?" he said.

"Hey, I been meaning to tell you that you got my gun from the other day." I pulled the nine out just enough to show it to him. "Mine's exactly like the one you gave me, only it's engraved. Where is it?"

"That bitch been gone. You know I don't keep no hot shit, and that shit was definitely hot," he said and went into the house, throwing me the dueces. That was my favorite gun, but I couldn't do much with it since it had been used to kill the manager at the motel.

CHAPTER 31

I rode real still all the way to Coco's house. With all that money in the trunk, I didn't want to get pulled over for nothing. I pulled into Coco's parking lot and called White Girl to open up the garage. My adrenaline had been so high at the anticipation of getting the money back in my possession that I had not thoroughly thought of a safe place to stash it. Even though Coco's crib was far from Fort Knox, I knew she was the only person I trusted who had a garage. I would sleep in the fucking car until Friday if need be, but I was glad to know I could finally relax since I at least had the money.

Just as the garage closed, White Girl came in through the door from the house. "Hey, girl. Wassup?" she asked, eating an apple.

"Wassuper," I said as I gave her a brief hug. We both walked back into the house, and I took a seat in the kitchen.

"Why you parking in the garage?" she asked.

"Because ever since I got out, I feel like I'm being followed," I lied. She didn't need to know what was in the trunk of the car until we got ready to make the trade on Friday.

"Oh, okay," she said and took a seat beside me.

"Where is Coco?" I asked.

"Out with her man that we have to go and meet in about… forty minutes," she said, glancing down at her watch, and then she tossed her finished apple into the trash.

"Damn. I forgot about that," I said.

"We gotta go or there will be hell to pay." She laughed.

"I know, I know." I laid my head down on the table. I really needed to hit the streets and meet up with the major money players I had planned to see first thing that morning, but somehow the day had gotten behind me.

"You okay, girl?" She rubbed my back.

"To be honest with you, no. I don't understand why my life is this complicated. I mean, the average twenty-five-year-old is not out there dealing with the things I deal with, and I'm tired of this. I just talked to Meechie, and he told me he was also taken in to the station for questioning the other day. I wonder why we got taken in and you didn't?" I asked, looking up at her.

"Lovely, I ain't going through this again. That nigga is trying to turn you against me because I'm on to his games and he know it. When this is all over, he's gonna make me go and holla at him on some real shit—no conversation and just my gun talking, and I mean that." She rolled her eyes.

"I don't know, but at this point, I don't even care no more. It's Wednesday, and we only got two days to go. Where is that money that you said you had?" I asked.

"Oh, I gotta go and pick it up first thing Friday morning because that's when my friend said he could have it." She smiled.

"Okay, girl. Let's go before we have to hear her mouth," I said, noticing that the time on the microwave said 4:35 p.m.

We got into White Girl's car and made our way downtown. We stopped at the light, and a man walked up to our car. He was carrying a sign that said, *"Why lie? I need a beer,"* and I burst out laughing.

"Girl, only in Detroit do you see some shit like this," she said, rolling down the window to give the man a ten.

"Ain't that the truth!" I agreed.

We pulled up in front of the Purple Room and gave the keys

to the valet. Just as we reached the door, a fine-ass, tall, cocky, brown-skinned dude came out. "Damn, baby. You looking good," he said to White Girl, who blushed.

"You don't look too bad yourself," she said back.

He was dressed in a pair of black slacks, a light blue Ralph Lauren button-up that was slightly rolled up, and a pair of shoes that looked like they were really expensive. Dude was looking real polished and clean cut.

"I'm William," he introduced himself. "I'm throwing a little soirée, and I was wondering if you and your girl would come and party with me and some of my friends tonight?" He handed us some sort of flyer out of his briefcase.

While they continued to flirt, I glanced over the flyer. It was black and white, with *"Detroit's Elite"* at the top. It said the party was going down that night at the Moet Lounge and that it was *"only for dons and divas"* who had that personal invitation.

"Sounds real official," White Girl said, and I guessed that she had also glanced at the flyer.

"It is, baby. When I do it, I do it big! I'm talking actors, athletes, city officials, and all." He smiled.

"Okay. We might check you out, William," she said, and we walked into the upscale restaurant/bar.

"Welcome to the Purple Room. How may I assist you?" asked a woman dressed in a silver silk blouse and a black pencil skirt.

"We are meeting our friend and her date," White Girl answered.

"Do you know where they're sitting?" she asked.

"No. Let me just call her real quick," I said. I pulled out my cell phone that was just starting to ring.

"Where the hell are you hoes?" Coco shouted.

"Chill. We are up here with the hostess, trying to find out where your ass is sitting," I said in a whispered tone. Yelling just wasn't the right thing to do in this kind of place.

"Oh." She changed her pitch. "I'm in the bathroom, but

De'Andre is sitting on the left side by the picture window across from the bar. I will be out in a minute, 'kay?" she said, and I hung up.

I repeated the instructions to the hostess, and she led us into the dining area and pointed us in the right direction. We walked past a few tables before we spotted him. He hadn't seen us yet, and that was a good thing.

"Oh shit! We need to get the fuck out of here right fucking now!" I backed up and bumped right into a waiter who was carrying a tray of food. As soon as the food hit the floor along with the fancy china and crystal that shattered, everybody turned our way, including De'Andre, who gout up out of his chair and started to approach us.

"Lovely, what's the matter?" White Girl asked as I grabbed her hand and ran to the exit.

"We got to get the fuck out of here," was all I said as Coco approached us.

"What is going on?" she asked.

"You need to come with us. You ain't safe here!" I screamed.

"But, L, I—" she started to complain.

"Coco, let's go!" I snapped, but she just stood there looking at me like I was crazy. I didn't have time to explain right then and there, so I asked her one last time to come with me. When she wouldn't cooperate, I did what I had to do and bounced, with White Girl in tow.

"You mind telling me what just happened in there?" White Girl asked as the valet brought the car to us.

Just as we got in, De'Andre flew through the restaurants doors and ran up to the valet to retrieve his ride as well.

"That is the same guy who was driving the bus that night when I had the run-in with my dad! I will never forget his tall ass with that slash across his face," I said as White Girl blew through a red light.

"Shit! Are you fucking serious?" she said and then sped up as the realness of what I was saying hit her.

"Lucifer played me," I spat just as my cell phone rang. "Hello?"

"Meet me at my house so you can tell me what happened," Coco said.

"Is De'Andre still with you?" I asked.

"No. When I went to apologize for what happened, he said it was okay and that he had an emergency come up so he would just see me in a little," she said in his defense.

"What is he driving?" I asked to make sure me and White Girl weren't being followed.

"A gray Expedition. Why?" she asked.

"I will see you when you get back to your house." I closed my phone and dropped it back in my purse. I checked for the Expedition all the way to Coco's house, and to my surprise, I didn't see one.

We ran into the house and flew up the stairs to retrieve the two guns White Girl had brought from home, but we couldn't find them anywhere.

"Shit!" I said after I flipped one of the mattresses over on its side.

"L, do you think she knew?" White Girl asked.

"What are you talking about?" I asked, feverishly checking the dresser drawers.

"Do you think Coco knew about De'Andre? What if she is the one setting you up? The snitch?"

Her words sounded crazy to me. Coco was my best friend in the world, and I knew it was all some kind of big misunderstanding, but before I had the opportunity to mention that, I heard the front door open.

"Lovely!" Coco called out my name.

"Up here!" I yelled down the stairs.

"Girl, what happened?" she asked as she entered the room.

"Did you fucking know your new man was the same one who

tried to help Lucifer kill her?" White Girl jumped right in.

"What?" Coco looked confused.

"Yeah, Coco. De'Andre works for my dad, and I don't think it's a coincidence that you two met. I think Lucifer was trying to use him to get to you and ultimately to me." I saw the hurt in her face, but the truth was the truth.

"Lovely, are you sure?" she asked.

"Unfortunately, yes. I will never forget a face like that."

"Wow. I knew it was too good to be true." She shook her head.

We all froze when the doorbell rang. We walked over to the window together and peeked through the blinds.

"Shit! This is about to get ugly," White Girl said.

I had to agree because standing outside was De'Andre.

"What should I do?" Coco asked with panic in her voice.

"Don't move. Maybe he will go away," I said.

White Girl smacked her lips. "Girl, he ain't leaving. We need to be prepared. Coco, where are those two guns I had in here?"

"Oh, I put them up in the attic with the money," she said and then went into the hallway and reached to pull the stairs down so White Girl could go and get them.

KNOCK…KNOCK…KNOCK…KNOCK

De'Andre beat on the door, and when no one answered, he started kicking the door. As big as he was, I knew one or two more good kicks, and the door was coming off.

"Lovely, he is coming in, girl. Let's all go up there," she said.

We tried to get up the stairs as quick as possible, but it was too late, because we heard the door cave in and crash to the floor. Coco jumped off the stairs and pushed it up, not completely closing it but making it look closed.

"White Girl, did you find them?" I whispered. I couldn't see her in the dark crawlspace, but I heard her fumbling around behind me.

"No, not yet," she said.

While she continued to search for our weapons, I tried my best to listen to what was going on downstairs, but I couldn't hear anything. I pressed the small opening further apart to give me a better view and a little sound.

"What the fuck took you so long?" he asked.

"I was in the bathroom," Coco said.

"Stop lying! Where is your girl at?"

"She ain't here," Coco lied for me.

"Bullshit! Where else would she be when the car she was riding in is sitting right outside?"

Hearing the aggravated voice, I turned back toward White Girl. "Fuck that! We gotta get down there before he hurt her or something," I said.

"We ain't going nowhere without a weapon," she said, still searching around.

"Why are you looking for her anyway? How in the fuck do you even know her?" Coco demanded.

"Baby, I will explain all that to you after I get your girl. I swear," he said just as White Girl told me she had found one of the guns.

With ease, we slid the stairs from the crawlspace down and quietly crept down the ladder with White Girl in front.

"For real, De'Andre, it's like that? So it's true then, huh? I been a part of the plan all along? So what, the three years we've been kickin' it and all those nights we spent together was for laughs? Was the proposal just for kicks too—some cruel-ass joke?" I heard Coco say, and I could tell her feelings were genuinely hurt.

"Uh, shortie, I'm telling you that it ain't shit like that, all right. Yes, I do work for Lucifer, and yes, kickin' it with you was part of the plan in the beginning, but I really did fall in love with you after the first year." He raised his right hand to the sky, like he was a Boy Scout swearing in.

"Bullshit!" Coco snapped just as we made it all the way down the stairs.

We crept down the hall past the kitchen, until we were standing a few feet away behind De'Andre's big ass.

"Baby, I swear I'm telling you the truth, and after I warn your girl about what's been going on, I'm leaving Lucifer's organization and getting the hell up outta here. I asked you to marry me because I want you and the kids to come with me," he said.

White Girl looked back at me, shaking her head.

"Well, then you tell me what's been going on, and I will give your message to her." Coco stood with her arms folded.

"Look, her peoples in on some bullshit, and they are coming for her. I been overhearing parts of the plan they have to kill her, and I just can't let her go out like that," he said.

I stopped in my tracks so I could hear every little detail about what he had to say. I tried to reach out for White Girl to stop, but she was out of my reach, still making her way into the living room.

"Be specific. What people are you talking about?" Coco asked.

The time went in slow motion as I waited for his response. Everyone in earshot was holding their breath except White Girl, who was almost right behind him. Just as he was about to open his mouth and speak, he must've sensed White Girl's presence, because he whipped around so fast that it scared the shit out of me. I guess it scared her, too, because instantly, she jumped and simultaneously squeezed the trigger, dropping De'Andre with one shot.

"Noooo!" Coco whined.

I looked on in awe. I couldn't believe how fast things had happened, and now there was a dead man stretched out in the middle of the floor. After a second, I regained my composure and immediately turned around to place the broken door back up in its frame. It wasn't closed by far, but it was enough to keep anyone in the parking lot from seeing the mayhem going on inside.

"Coco, I'm so sorry. I swear I didn't mean to. It just...just slipped," White Girl said as she knelt down beside Coco, who was pounding on ol' boy's chest like that would bring him back. Shit, at that point, the only revivin' his ass would've been Jesus.

"Damn. If it ain't one thing, it's another," I said, sitting down on the floor next to my girls.

"L, word to my daughter I didn't mean to." She looked over at me with a tear-stained face.

I didn't have the words she needed to hear at the moment, so I just inhaled and shook my head.

"Please get up, baby. Get up!" Coco said, and I patted her back. "Lovely, are we going to jail?" Coco looked up at me with horror in her eyes.

"No, Coco. Ain't nobody going to jail, girl," I answered, more confident than I actually felt. Truth was, I didn't know what to do. For all I knew, the police could have been surrounding this muthafucka right then. Normally I would call Meechie and let him handle it, but the way I left his ass that afternoon, he wouldn't have pissed on me to put a fire out.

"Look, y'all go and get y'all stuff. L, you take her back to your room. I made this mess, and I'll clean it up." White Girl stood up from the floor.

"How?" I asked.

"Just trust me and get Coco outta here. I got this. The hook ain't coming, but if they do, I will take the heat. I will just say I feared for my life and thought he was breaking in when he kicked the door in, so I shot his ass," she replied like she had it all figured out.

I didn't remind her that she was behind him when she shot him and that it would not be considered self-defense. I didn't want to kill her drive to handle the situation, so I picked Coco up off the floor, and we went to retrieve her stuff since mine was already at the Marriott.

CHAPTER 32

"How could she, Lovely?" Coco wanted to know.

I didn't know what to say that would bring her any peace, so I opted to just keep quiet and let her vent.

"I mean, he wasn't even there to get you. He just wanted to warn you, but she shot him." She cried some more, and I handed her a tissue from my purse.

I surveyed the scene as I backed out of the garage. *So far so good.* I sort of had an attitude about having to drive my rental with all that money in the trunk, but I couldn't leave it there, so away we pulled with millions. I knew the hotel I was staying in didn't have a covered parking structure or any twenty-four-hour security or even a valet, so I decided to head to the MGM Casino and get a room there.

Fifteen minutes later, we arrived at the MGM, and Coco was still sobbing like a newborn baby. "Come on, girl," I said. "We're here." The valet walked up to my door, and I grabbed my purse and pulled out $200. "Please, please, PLEASE watch out for my car and make sure nothing happens to it, and I swear I will look out for you." I handed the hefty tip to the thirty-something man.

"No doubt, ma'. I got you on the real, doe." He took my keys and the money and pulled off into the parking area designated for valet-parked cars.

I didn't want to walk away, but with the car behind me honking because I was blocking the path, I had no choice. I put my arm around Coco's shoulder, and we walked into the lobby. It was definitely an upgrade from where I was staying, and I knew it would come with a hefty price tag, but it was worth it for the security.

"Hello, ladies. How may I assist you? Ooh, girl! That bag is fierce," an obviously gay clerk asked as we approached the reception desk.

I read his gold nametag. "Phillip, I need a room for three nights." I took my hand from around Coco's shoulder and reached inside my purse, ready to pay the piper.

"Aw…man problems?" he said and gave us a pouty face before he looked at the reservation computer. "Girl, sometimes they make you want to kill them," he added, and Coco started wailing all over again.

"Damn! Now why'd you have to go and say that?" was what I wanted to say, but instead I just rubbed Coco's back and smiled at him politely while I waited for the price of the room.

"I'm sorry, honey. I didn't know that was going to upset you. Don't worry. He will be calling you in a day or two, wanting to kiss and make up." He smiled, and Coco turned it up some more.

"Listen, Phillip, man, I know you trying to help, but I really just need to get her up to the room to lie down. What's the ticket?" I asked.

"Oh, I understand. Um…" He looked back at the computer screen. "We only have the luxury corner suites available tonight. Those run $503.19 a night after tax. Would you like one of those?" He looked up at me, bright eyed.

"Yeah, I guess I have no other choice," I said and gave him fifteen hundreds and a ten.

He took down my information, gave me my change and a key-card, along with my receipt, and pointed us toward the elevator.

The whole ride up to the fourth floor, I thought about how I would get the rest of the money I needed the next day. I knew my girl was going through something, but I swear I was hoping her ass would settle down for a nap so I could dip and get what I needed before the whole day was lost.

"Man, I can't believe he is gone," Coco said as we walked inside the plush room.

It was something straight off HGTV, with bold neutral colors and décor. I dropped my purse on the beige coffee table and then rolled Coco's suitcase into the bedroom across from the living room. "Coco, I don't know what to say, boo." I set her suitcase down and turned back into the living room, taking a seat next to her on the mustard-yellow loveseat.

"Do you think that bitch shot him on purpose?" She wiped her eyes and sat back.

"It all happened so fast that I don't know what to think," I said honestly, because I didn't. "What happened today could've happened to anybody. Those guns are nothing to play with, and I think she just wanted to scare him, but when he whipped around, he scared her, and her knee-jerk reaction was to squeeze the trigger." I sat back with her because I was exhausted. It seemed like every day that I woke up in Detroit, the drama just got worse and worse. At that point, I couldn't worry about what had already happened, though, because all my thoughts were on what in the hell could possibly happen next.

"Now what am I going to do, girl?" She sighed.

I turned to face her. "You are going to pick up the pieces and keep it pushing. Coco, you've been my best friend since I can remember, and the one thing I know about you is that you a survivor. That nigga wasn't your everything, and shit coulda gone way different today." She looked at me, so I continued, "What if he was out to get me and he shot you for trying to cover for me? Shit, we really don't know what his intentions were. All we know fo' sho is that he was working for Lucifer, and that speaks volumes," I said matter of factly and rested my case.

"You right, girl. My ass is tripping." She rubbed her face.

I smiled and was about to get up and pour us a shot of Patron from the bar in the corner when my cell phone rang. "It's Maine," I thought since my screen said *"out of area."* I flipped my phone open. "Hey, baby."

"Hey yourself," Nichols responded, and I laughed.

"I thought you were my man, Mrs. Nichols?" I said, and she laughed too.

"Girl, speaking of your man, he got into a scuffle with another prisoner, and they got him on lockdown, so he can't call you tonight."

"What happened?" I asked, not really worried that my man was hurt because Maine was from the school of hard knocks. I knew he could use his fists just as well as—if not better than—he could use a gun.

"I'm not so sure on the details, but I do know the other guy had to see a doctor."

I could tell she was smiling, and that made me smile too.

"I'm 'bout to take a shower," Coco mouthed, and I nodded. She walked into the room and closed the door behind her.

I stretched out on the sofa to get comfortable. "I can't wait until he comes home," I said, imagining how the day would go in my head.

"I know you can't, sweetie. Have you made contact with your dad?" she asked, taking me out of my daydream.

"Yes, and he is supposed to meet me at the club tomorrow in the VIP room. Do you have everything set up on your end?" I wanted to know. I had given her the venue detail the other day, and she was supposed to set up the club with various cameras and voice recorders for the surveillance team.

"Yes, my end is tight. Just make sure everything goes off without a hitch. We don't want him to know we are on to him," she added.

"Yeah, I know," I said. *You Feds are the least of his worries,* I thought to myself. Frankie was gonna put him six feet under, and there wasn't shit he would be able to do about it. As we talked some more, I filled her in on the remaining details, and then my line clicked. I looked at the caller ID and saw that it was White Girl. I told Nichols to holla back at me later, and then I clicked over. "You good?"

"Yeah, I'm good. Where y'all at?" she asked in a tone I couldn't read.

"We got a room at MGM. You handle that?"

"Yeah, it's handled. I cleaned up and grabbed my shit," she said.

I could hear the wind blowing in the background. "Damn, that was fast," I said and looked at the time on my phone. It had only been an hour and a half. I had never disposed of a body, and I thought it would be a longer process, but I guess she knew better than me, so I let it go.

"Yeah, I had some help, but it's done. Is she still mad?" she asked, concern filling her voice.

"She will be all right. You know Coco will be on to the next one tomorrow at the club, so don't stress about that. Just get your ass over here." I gave her the room number and told her I would see her in a few. As soon as I hung up, I was about to pour another shot, but my cell phone rang again, Tiny this time. "What up, girl?"

"Hey, I'm up here at the club getting everything together. It's beautiful, girl. I even found some of the girls from the Rump Shaker to come and dance on the poles off the main stage." She was so excited.

"Tiny, you know, you should leave all the scheming behind and start an event planning business." The girl was talented, and I knew she could start a very lucrative business that didn't involve opening her legs for some paper.

"Lovely, you know I ain't the average girl. My own business sounds good, but I ain't got time for that. It's much easier to just fuck the businessmen and spend their money, don't you think?" She let out an evil laugh.

"God bless the woman that got her own," I said, and she got my drift.

"Anyway, I will swing by tomorrow, and we can all get ready for the party together."

"Okay. We at the MGM, so call me when you on the way, and I'll give you the room number," I said, and we ended the call.

I stood to finally get my shot of Patron, and I'd damned if there wasn't another interruption—this time a knock at the door. I walked over to the peephole and saw White Girl standing there with her middle finger right in my view. I swung the door open. "Bitch, your ass ain't got no manners."

CHAPTER 33

It was six o'clock in the morning when Coco and White Girl finally dropped for the night. We were up talking and drinking everything off the bar. The good news was that Coco was no longer mad at White Girl; the bad news was that my ass still had to come up with the rest of the money. I had let those hoes talk me into relaxing, and now I was a day late and over $400,000 short. "Shit!" I cursed to myself as I sat up on the couch, anticipating my next move. I picked up the empty pizza box off the table and took it over to the trash in the small kitchen. My eyes burned, and I was sleepy as hell, but I had too much to do, so I headed to the shower. Sleep was the last thing on my list.

I got in and turned the water on full blast. It felt wonderful, but then my cell phone rang again. I sighed loudly, knowing that the much-needed shower would have to turn into a ho bath. I washed up quickly and stepped out. I dried off and went for my cell phone on the counter; it was Do It. I called him back, but it went straight to voicemail twice, so I put the phone down and went to look in Coco's bag for something to wear since my clothes were still at the Marriott. As I rummaged through her stuff, my phone rang again, and this time I caught it before the call ended, "Hey, I tried to hit you back," I said, pulling out a black Hanes female wife-beater and a pair of light denim skinny jeans. I wasn't into wearing other people's panties, so my ass went alfresco.

"That's funny. I don't remember giving you my number," the caller said.

I didn't have to ask who it was to know that it was Frankie's goon. "Today is the day," I said with a smirk on my face.

"So what's the plan?" he asked, cutting right to the chase.

"LB will be in the back of a Fed car, and I will be behind them."

"A Fed car? What type of shit are you smoking?"

"Listen, there is nothing I can do about that. His ass will be in their custody, so we have to go through them to get to him. The route they will take runs into Greenfield near Ten Mile. You and your team will be there, dressed as construction workers, and someone will tell the driver that there is a detour. You will instruct them to go through an alley, and that will be where the magic will happen," I said, giving him just enough without incriminating myself.

"All right. So where are we going to get this construction get-up?" he questioned.

"At noon, call 313-555-5897," I said, rattling off Tiny's number. She was already up on the game, and she had everything ready to roll. She was doing a man that owned his own construction business, and he agreed to let us borrow some of his stuff for the night.

"Okay. Well, it seems like you have it all planned out, so I guess we will be seeing you tonight then," he said.

"My girl will give you the specifics...and make sure my niece is there."

"She will be there, and you will have her as soon as I get what I came for." With that, he ended the call.

I put on a pair of Coco's black and pink Reeboks, grabbed my keys, and headed out.

My first stop was to get my stuff and check out of the Marriott. I drove White Girl's car for obvious reasons, and when I pulled up in front of the hotel, I whipped right into the first handicap parking space I saw. I normally wouldn't do that, but it wasn't a normal day, and the quicker I got in, the quicker I could get out. I left my purse in the car and flew inside, bumping right into Vilan.

"Damn. Where is the fire?" he asked.

"My bad," I said and then moved around him like an NBA player on a cross-up.

"I'll be watching you tonight at your party, Ms. Brown," he said from behind me.

I was too focused to pay him any attention. I pressed the elevator button, but it seemed to take entirely too long, so I opted for the stairs. I reached my floor and the room door in no time, grabbed my stuff, threw it in the bag, and scanned the room for anything I might've missed. I didn't see anything, so I was back out of the room and down the stars in no time. I practically jogged up to the car and smacked my lips when I saw the ticket in the windshield of the car; I knew it was from Vilan's ass. I opened the door and tossed my stuff over into the passenger seat, cranked the engine, and started to pull out. Of course my phone rang. "Yeah?" I answered, out of breath.

"Lo, swing by here when you get a chance," Do It said.

I glanced at the clock on the dashboard. I really didn't have time to be shooting the breeze that day and was about to tell him that, but then I remembered he said he had something for me. I didn't know what it was, but I was a little curious, and I was only right down the street. "Be there in five," I said and hung up.

I pulled into the driveway and threw the car in park while jumping out at the same time. I knocked on the white door lightly, and it opened right up.

"Hey, Lovely," Lisa said as she stood to the side so I could enter.

"Hey, Lisa. My brother called me. Is it okay that I'm here this early?" I asked. It was only seven thirty in the morning, far too early for visiting hours.

"Girl, you know it's okay for you. You want some breakfast?" she asked, walking in to the kitchen in pajamas instead of scrubs.

"No, I'm good. Thanks though. Uh, you sleep here?" I wanted to know.

"Normally we rotate, but for the most part, since I'm co-owner, yeah. My house is only four doors down, so I'm basically here all the time." She shrugged. "He is in the back waiting for you."

I smiled at her and went on my way down the hall to Do It's room. I walked right in since the door was open. "What up, gangsta?" I asked, leaning down to hug him.

He was sitting in his chair looking out the window, in deep thought. "What up, Lo. Close that door for me," he said.

I did, then walked back over to and sat on the chair next to him.

"I got three duffel bags on the floor in that closet." He weakly pointed his finger to a closet on my left. "The last time we counted, there was $600,000 altogether. I want you to take it and get my daughter back," he said.

I stared at him in amazement. "Where did you get that much money from, Do It?"

"The second time we went to the old house, we started looking around for things I might have left behind that could remind me of anything. We were checking the closets, and they were taped up in a box marked 'baby stuff'. Me and Lisa brought them back here. I been pinching here and there, but like I said, the last time we counted, there was 600 thou'." He squinted from the sun beaming through his bedroom window.

I sat silent for a minute, as it all came together. Do It was fresh to death because he ass had stacks on deck. "Wow," was all I could say before I got up and grabbed the three bags and placed them on the bed. I unzipped them one at a time. They all smelled like money, and there was nothing but Franklins looking back at me. "Damn. I could kiss yo' ass right now." I smiled from ear to ear. He didn't know how much relief he had just given me. "I'ma get her back, bro, and when I do, I'm going to bring her straight to you," I said.

He hesitated and then nodded. "I would like that."

"It's time for you to come home. You know that, right?" I asked.

He nodded.

"Get ready, because tonight when this is over, I will be here with a U-haul."

"Who's moving?" Lisa said as she walked inside with a plate of turkey bacon and scrambled eggs.

"Lo wants me to move back home with family," he said, not looking up at her. I could tell he was attached to her and didn't want to see the hurt in her eyes.

"Well, DeShawn, I guess we knew this day would one day come, huh?" She looked deflated. "What about his treatments though?" she asked.

I smiled. "Oh, we have the best in the business," I said, and she frowned.

"The best, huh? And who might that be?" She looked at me with jealousy all over her face.

"I think she goes by the name of Lisa." I laughed, and she smiled. "I know you're the co-owner of this place, but would your sister get mad if we took you with us?" I asked as Do It's eyes lit up.

"I will talk with her and let you know," she said, and I hoped the sister would agree.

"Okay. I will see you later. I need to go and get breakfast for Mr. Henry." She walked out of the room, leaving me and Do It alone.

"Sis, call me the minute you get my daughter back. I will be praying for your safety. Tell her that Daddy ain't perfect, but he can't wait to meet her."

"Do It, Shawnie is a kid, and her love is unconditional. Perfect or not, you are her daddy, and that's more than enough." I hugged my brother, kissed him on the cheek, and grabbed the bags to leave.

CHAPTER 34

The time had finally come, and I was scared to death, but the show had to go on. I applied the finishing touches to my lip gloss, sprayed some Juicy Couture, and slipped into my gold strapless, custom-made Roberto Cavalli exclusive that fit me like a glove, courtesy of my main man James Backwards, who was sent by Maine. He had showed up to my room door equipped with all the necessities, and I was thankful. I looked red carpet ready, and you can believe I was feeling myself too. Coco had done my hair in a bunch of loose spiral curls that hung down the back with the extensions she added. She also hooked my eyelashes up and arched the hell out of my eyebrows. My fingernails were polished in metallic gold and done in minx, the same as my toes, and my make-up was flawless. Thank God my face had cleared up!

I had just sat down on the bed to put on my gold Balenciaga stiletto sandals when my phone rang. "Hello?" I said into it without looking at the ID. As soon as I heard the operator, I smiled and pressed one immediately. "Hey, baby."

"Wassup, boo. Did you like your surprise?"

"You know I did, Maine. Thank you, baby. I wish you could see me." I smiled

"Me too, boo. Tonight is the night. You ready?" he asked.

"Yes. I'm nervous and excited at the same time, but I can't wait until tomorrow for you to come home. We are going on a vacation right after we get married," I said and then turned to my left to put on my jewelry that was sitting on the bed beside me.

"You can do it, baby. I wish I was there to support you, but I know that you got this."

We talked a few more minutes, and then it was time for me to go. I stood in the mirror, took one last look, grabbed my clutch, and left my room. I crossed the hall and knocked on Tiny's room door. She had rented a room that day, and Coco and White Girl were over there at the pre-celebration "Let's party, my nigga!" she said, swinging the door open and hitting me with a strong whiff of weed.

"Smell like y'all already partying." I laughed.

She, White Girl, and Tiny walked into the hallway, looking fierce as ever in their different shades of gold. White Girl was dressed in a gold one-piece with flare legs; it really looked good up against her skin tone. Coco was dressed in a shiny sequined baby doll dress, and Tiny had on some type of copper-gold bodysuit with designer fishnets—definitely an outfit that was hard to pull off, but girlfriend was working it.

We walked outside just as the gold stretch Hummer pulled up. Once we were inside the vehicle, the private party got started big time. There was Patron and Don Julio already on ice, and we took shot after shot until both bottles were empty. Hell, I don't know how the rest of them were feeling, but I was bent by the time we pulled up to the party. My head was spinning, but at least my nerves were calm.

The driver opened the door, and I saw a line wrapped down two city blocks. "Damn, Tiny! You did your thing," I said as we walked up to the backdrop, which had the theme *"Diamonds and Gold,"* with one of my pictures from the photo shoot. We posed for about four pictures, and then we walked inside. The place was absolutely beautiful. It had an ice sculpture, a chocolate fountain, a five-tier cake, and more. The crowd was hyped up, and the dance floor was packed. "Girl, this place is already full! I don't know how those people outside are going to get in," I said to White Girl, who nodded.

"I just got word that the number one stunna herself has just entered the building, Lovely, we see you, baby!" the DJ called out.

Tiny escorted us up the stairs, where a security guard was standing. She whispered something in his ear, and he gave her four silver wristbands. We put them on and went up the stairs to the glass VIP room, which was guarded by another security person in front of the door; this one was a woman. We showed our bands, and she nodded, letting me and my girls in the room and closing the door behind us.

CHAPTER 35

I watched from the VIP as my girls did the bad-girl hustle out on the dance floor. They tried to get me to go, but I needed to stay focused on what was about to go down. Just as I waved at Coco, who was waving at me, I heard a tap at the door. Walking over to it I called out, "Who is it?" I thought that the room was a bit of a stupid concept; the whole damn room was see through except for the damn door.

"It's the man of the hour," I heard, causing my heart to skip a beat or two.

With a shaking hand, I opened the door and put on my best poker face. The security guard walked in.

"He has on a silver band, ma'am, so that means he is on your VIP guest list."

"Yes, it's fine," I said and closed the door. I walked over to the black leather sofa behind Lucifer, taking a seat just as he did. "Would you like a drink?" I asked.

"No thanks. I just really want to get down to business, if you don't mind my being blunt." He sat back and crossed his legs like a true old-school playa. I sat back as well and took him all in. He was dressed in a pair of beige linen pants; a tan, white, and gold summer cashmere sweater; a beige Kangol cap; and beige pair of Stacy Adams loafers, trimmed in gold.

"Okay, that's not a problem," I said and then went into my script. "So, now that I'm back in Detroit and—"

He cut me off with a raised hand. "Cut the bullshit, okay, Lovely? Tell me the real reason you asked me to come here," he ordered.

"No bullshit—just business," I said, trying to keep my cool.

"Lovely, I been in the game since before you was born. People don't exactly invite their so-called enemies to a party and offer them a hookup," He said, making air quotations.

"Well, if that's what you thought this is, then why'd you show your face?" I wanted to know.

"For the show, baby."

"What show?" I asked.

"Your finale!" He laughed a wicked laugh, and it made me very uneasy.

Just as I was about to ask what he meant by that, the VIP door opened. "It's too crowded in the building. We been shut down by the fire marshal," the security guard said.

Lucifer went over to the glass and peered out into crowd, and I followed him. The crowd was being directed outside. Lucifer glanced over at me, and I'm sure he wondered if it was part of some kind of plan.

"Come on," said the guard with urgency.

"I can't believe this bullshit," I said with attitude as I grabbed my purse.

We followed her down the stairs, and she led us out the side door to the alley.

"Well, I guess I will have to catch the show some other time," he said with a cocky smirk on his face.

That look was quickly replaced with utter shock when Agent Nichols, my security guard in a wig and sunglasses, said, "Lavelle Lucifer Brown, I have waited all this time to tell you that you are under arrest. You have the right to remain…"

While she read him his Mirandas, he started screaming, "I

should've killed you when I had the chance, you fucking rat! You are a fucking coward, Lovely! Do you hear me? A coward!"

I waved at him as Nichols put him in the back of a black Navigator. "I guess tonight was *your* finale," I said with a huge smile on my face.

"Your ending is coming, baby—real soon. Believe that. Everybody that smiles in your face ain't always your friend. Remember that. Every eye ain't always closed, and every goodbye ain't always gone." He winked as Nichols pushed his door closed.

"Lovely, thank you again for what you've done for me. I know you have a lot of other things going on, so it means a lot that you also found the time to keep your word to me," she said, grabbing me in a tight hug.

"Mrs. Nichols, I'm glad I could do it. I hope you can retire and live in peace now. Don't forget to come over for dinner sometime, now that this is behind us," I said.

"Oh, baby, I will, and it's all thanks to you. You be careful, girl. You hear me?"

"Yes, ma'am. I will. Now, go get my man and make sure you're both at the banquet hall I reserved at the MGM tomorrow at noon," I said and then made my way down the alley to my awaiting rental car with White Girl behind the wheel.

I got in, and she took off behind the Navigator as it pulled out of the alley. "I hope everything is in place," she said.

"So far so good. The fire marshal thing worked out, so everything else should go off without a hitch," I said, reaching in the glove compartment to get my .357 revolver with hollow-point bullets. "Frankie should have someone call me right about now," I said, and the phone rang right on point. "Everything in place at the detour?" I asked.

"We're ready and waiting," he said.

CHAPTER 36

We followed the Navigator as it bent a few corners and finally came to the expected roadblock. There was construction equipment set up, and a big orange sign that said *"CAUTION! Workers below ground."* A construction worker walked over to the Navigator and pointed over to the right. There were a few words exchanged before the Navigator slowly turned in the direction of the detour. We pulled into the deserted warehouse parking lot, blocking the entrance from the alley, and the Navigator turned around to face us. "What are you doing?" the driver asked as he rolled the window down.

White Girl had rolled her window down as well. "Those construction workers told me this is the detour, but I don't think they know what they are talking about, do you?" She smiled.

"No, I don't think so either, but if you want to follow me, I will take you back the other way toward the freeway." The man smiled back.

I scanned the lot for Frankie, who should've been there by now, but there was no sign of him or his people.

"Okay, but can I ask you one more thing?" she said.

I looked at her strangely because she had strayed away from the plan.

"Sure," the man said just as White Girl jumped from the car

with her gun out.

"Put your fucking hands where I can see them!" She opened up his door, and he got out with his hands up.

Right then and there, I knew she had lost her damn mind, because she shot the Fed escort point blank in the head. "What the fuck?!" I yelled. I climbed over the seat and was about to throw it in reverse, but I felt the cold steel up against the side of my face, stopping me in my tracks.

"Where you think you going?" the person asked, and it sent chills up my spine because it was the same voice I'd come to know as Meechie.

Damn! What the fuck is up? I wondered as he opened my door. I concealed my gun as best I could in my small clutch bag.

"Get out now," he said, and I did as I was told. He instructed me to walk toward the back of the Navigator, and I did, praying for a small miracle with every step.

"White Girl, what the fuck is this?" I looked at her, standing there with a smirk on her face.

"I told you I'd showed up for your finale, baby." Lucifer got out of the truck laughing hysterically, still handcuffed.

"Lovely, I hate to tell you this, but your paranoid ass was right the whole time. Your circle ain't tight and never has been!" she said with a hardy laugh. "See, your daddy is my mentor. He got me started in the dope game, putting me on with cocaine, and he had me on his payroll long before you did, LB. He gave me a mission when I was released from jail to take over the streets with a product he could brand as his own and to get his throne ready for him when he broke out." She smiled. "As fate would have it, Tori was killed the same night, and you basically threw the position right in my lap when you decided to join the game. The day I was kidnapped after my baby shower, that was all in the plans, and my water breaking made it all the more believable." She laughed again. "Lucifer was supposed to take you down that night and become your alias LB, and then me, Do It, and our daughter were out of there."

"There is no way my brother was part of this sick-ass plan of yours," I said, unable to believe what was happening.

"No, but had you been killed, he would've had no other choice but to leave with me and live happily ever after. But you messed that all up when you let him die, now didn't you?" She mean-mugged me. "Anyway, after he got killed, I had no choice but to go with you and Maine when y'all came and got me out of the hospital. I been planning this out for five long years, and I'm glad this shit is over."

"So this whole Shawnie thing is bogus?" I asked.

"Yep! I had her kidnapped because I knew that was the only way for me to get a payday out of you," she said.

"So all this is about fuckin' money?" I wanted to know.

"Hell yeah!" she said. "See, the plan was to kidnap Shawnie for ransom, the sum of six mill to be exact, using this whole Frankie beef to my advantage. Once I got it, I would leave in the middle of the night, never to be seen or heard from again, but shit went to the left when that Fed came and took Maine to jail." I tried to comprehend what she was saying, but something wasn't adding up."

"Wait…if you work for him," I said, pointing at my sorry excuse for a father, "why did you pretend to have Frankie's guy call saying he wanted LB on a platter?" I stared at her in disbelief.

"Good question, girl." She smiled, and I could tell Lucifer didn't even know about that part of her demented plan. "See, your dad has old money, and I want it! My partner and I played both sides against the middle, and we are leaving this muthafucka millionaires, thanks to you and this old stupid muthafucka. Now, you come stand over here with yo' daddy," she instructed, motioning me with her gun.

"So this whole time you been working with Meechie?"

"Yeah. We kept yo' ass dizzy, didn't we? I had you thinking it was him, and he had you thinking it was me—and it was both of us all along. Now, the only question is which one of you should I kill first?" She paced back and forth.

"Really, Candace? After all I've done for you, this is how you repay me?" Lucifer asked.

"Hell yeah! Shit, you was the one to teach me never to pass up an opportunity when you see a nigga slipping. Remember that?" She stopped and stared at him.

"I was also the one who taught you to never bite the hand that feeds you, bitch!" He spat in her direction.

While they continued their bickering, I tried to get a good grip on the handle of my gun through my purse.

"Lucifer, it's been a pleasure, but your fucking time is up. Any last words?" she asked.

My heartbeat quickened. I had contemplated this moment over and over, but I still wasn't ready—especially not like this. I looked at Lucifer, and for the first time in a long time, I saw an apology in his eyes. He didn't have to verbally say he was sorry, because the way he looked at me told it all. My eyes watered up, and I could've sworn his did too.

"Meechie, you ain't shit, and you ain't never gon' be shit but a fucking low-rate hustle man. White Girl, your ass can suck my dick. You will never be as good as I was…never!" His voice raised an octave. "Lovely," he said as his eyes fell back on me, "baby girl, I guess Daddy will see you in the next lifetime. Hopefully there, things will be different." He squared his shoulders up like a soldier, walked right up to White Girl, and placed his forehead up against the barrel of her gun. "Pull the fucking trigger!"

BOOM!

I watched as my father's body hit the ground. Blood stained his outfit instantly, and I sobbed silently. It's funny: When people do things to hurt us, we get so mad that we couldn't care less if they are dead or alive, but the minute they take that final breath, we think of several reasons why whatever we were mad about just really wasn't that serious in the first place. We think of what we wish we had said before that fateful last moment. God says, "Nobody knows the time nor the hour," but I knew Lucifer's time was up just like he did, and I should've said something. If I had been granted a repeat, I would've said, *"Daddy, I love you, and I forgive you. I know everyone can't be an angel. When things go wrong and life doesn't turn out right, you resort to doing what you have to do to survive. You were a lost soul whose intentions started off good, I'm sure, but through bad judgment and wrong decisions, you became a monster who will always be misunderstood."*

"All right. Your turn." She pointed her smoking gun at me like it was nothing.

"Where is Shawnie?" I wanted to know because my soul wouldn't rest in the afterlife, no matter where I ended up, if I didn't know that child was safe.

"She's at my mama's house."

"Uh, before you smoke her, I got something to say," Meechie said, snatching my clutch out of my hand. He reached inside and raised my own gun to me, but to my amazement, he also raised his shotgun, which was in his other hand, to White Girl.

"What the fuck, Meechie?" she asked with a look of disbelief.

"See, what neither of you bitches know is that I been waiting for this day to come for a very long time. Remember when I told you I had a son who was killed?" he asked.

I nodded.

"The streets called my boy 'Spooky'," he said.

It felt like the weight of the world dropped down on top of my chest. I looked at White Girl, who looked like she had just seen a ghost.

"He had a security camera on his front porch, and I saw the tape of you two bitches setting him up. White Girl, you seduced him out on the porch, and Lovely, you hid in the shadows. I also saw Do It posted up across the street in your Range Rover. I played shit cool and didn't say nothing because I knew I was going to make all three of you muthafuckas pay. That night, you called me and asked if I wanted to buy your last package so you could get out of town. I knew I had to act fast, so I called Do It and asked him where y'all was at and if it would be easier for me to just come out there and pick it up. He told me it would and gave me the info. I pulled up and went into beast mode. I yanked that nigga out the car, put him in my whip, and drove off. I was the one who called you and told you to say your last words, and then I shot that nigga!"

"You killed the love of my life!" White Girl screamed, and I just looked on in silence because it was all finally making sense.

"I would've killed you bitches, too, but you got away until White Girl's money-hungry ass called me with this little plan of hers and I knew I couldn't resist." Without warning, he shot White Girl in the chest, blowing flesh and bone and blood everywhere.

I took that as my cue to run for it. I didn't care if he caught me in the back or not. Shit, I wasn't no dumb chick by far, and my ass wasn't going to stand there and wait for my turn. I didn't get more then seven steps before I heard the shot that was supposed to end my life, but fate intervened, and I was tackled to the ground by a person I didn't even see because shit was happening too fast. I hit my head on the concrete, and things became blurry as I got dizzy. I saw flashing lights and people running past me.

"Officer down! I need a bus!" someone screamed.

I slowly sat up and tried to focus on what was taking place. Mrs. Nichols was lying on the ground next to me with blood covering her shoulder. She must've been the one to tackle me. Then I looked up at the commotion taking place behind me.

"Lovely, you are going down, bitch! I swear on my son's grave!" Meechie screamed as the federal agents hemmed him up and placed handcuffs on him.

"It looks like you missed," I said as I stood and checked my body for wounds. Aside from my head, there were none.

"Naw, bitch. I always keep a backup plan. You are going down. I already put Plan B in motion."

EPILOGUE

The day was perfect, and there was no way I could be any happier. It was my wedding day, and I couldn't get down the aisle fast enough. I still hadn't seen Maine since he had been released, but I knew he would be ready and waiting to make me his wife. I couldn't sleep at all the night before, partly because I was up thinking about how conniving both White Girl and Meechie had been. I mean I really didn't see that coming, but I'm glad it was over and they both ended up getting what they deserved. The other reason I couldn't sleep was simple: I was up kissing and hugging all over my little Shawnie. She was safe and finally back where she belonged. I don't know how I will explain what happened to her mother, but I will stress over that later.

On a positive note, I was able to convince Do It to come to the wedding so everyone could see him, and he was also still onboard to let me introduce him to Shawnie. *I hope she handles this well. The poor girl has already been through too damn much,* I thought to myself as I stood from the chair and smoothed out my money-green Chanel dress. I gave myself a once-over and was about to go and do the damn thing when there came a knock at the door. "Come in!" I called out.

"Oh, don't you look beautiful?" Agent Nichols said as she walked into the room wearing a navy-blue Yves Saint Laurent pantsuit.

"No, you're the one looking good…and I see those red-bottom shoes too," I said, pointing to her Christian Louboutin heels.

"Well, this old girl still got it, and I can flaunt it now that I'm officially retired." She did a spin, and I clapped. "Do I have on the right color?" she asked.

I nodded. I had told my few guests that this was not a traditional wedding and to wear their best money green or navy blue that they had, which were our favorite colors. "I'm so glad you are okay, and I can't stress enough how thankful I am that you jumped in front of that bullet for me," I said, telling the whole truth and nothing but the truth.

"Lovely, I keep telling you it was nothing. I'm just sorry for you that things played out the way they did." She rubbed my shoulder.

"Yeah, but I just have to keep it moving I guess." I shrugged.

The door opened, and in came Coco, her two boys, Shawnie, and Do It. "I told you to knock! You just don't be opening up doors," Coco snapped at Corey.

He did a U-turn and ran out of the room with his brother in tow. "Ugh! This is girl's stuff in here," they said, and I laughed.

"I'll be out front," Nichols said, and I gave her a hug.

"Auntie L, you look so pretty! Will I be like you when I grow up?" she asked.

I smiled. "No, baby. You will be better than me, and I will make sure of that."

"Where is my mommy? I can't find her anywhere." She looked around the small makeshift dressing room.

I took a deep breath and bent down before her. "Baby, your mom has gone to Heaven to be with God." *At least I hope so anyway.*

"So who will be my mommy now?" she asked after thinking it over.

"I don't know, baby, but I do know that God has given you

a daddy in place of your mommy," I said and grabbed Do It's hand.

She looked up at him, just staring into his eyes, and then she reached up and rubbed his face like it was the most natural thing in the world.

A tear slipped down my cheek, and I glanced up and saw Coco wiping her own tears away.

"Will you leave me, too, even though I have a daddy now?" She turned her attention back to me, and I shook my head vigorously.

"No, baby. Not ever! You will always have Auntie L and Uncle Maine. You and your daddy will stay with us until he is all well, okay?" I said.

She smiled. "You promise?"

"I promise," I said and stuck out my pinky finger for a pinky promise, making it official.

"Shawnie, do you want to ride on Daddy's wheelchair?" Do It asked, and Shawnie hopped up there, ready to roll. I laughed as the two of them sped out the room and down the hallway.

"You ready, boo?" Coco asked.

"Let's do it, bestie." I put my arm around her shoulder, and we made our way to my destiny.

* * *

"I know that he loves me because he told me so…I know that he loves me because his feelings show and when he looks at me his brown eyes tell his soul!" Beyoncé crooned from the sound system as I made my way toward the aisle. I glanced around the nearly bare room with only a few chairs and an altar and realized it didn't matter to me that there were only a handful of people there to partake in my special day. What mattered was that those in attendance genuinely loved and cared for me. As I walked toward the altar, I smiled at Nichols, then at Do It, and finally rested my eyes upon my king. He was decked out in a blue prison outfit that resembled hospital scrubs and a blue blazer, with a huge grin

on his face. He must've noticed me checking out his gear, so he mouthed that he didn't have time to get anything else. I smiled and mouthed back that it didn't matter because I loved him just the way he was.

I'm not going to lie, my mind was all over the place, as the minister I'd just found in the Yellow Pages that morning talked about the sanctity of marriage. I couldn't wait to get back to the room to start making babies.

"Miss," he said, and I looked at him. "Do you have vows?"

"Oh, yes. I'm sorry," I said, and everybody laughed. I cleared my throat. I didn't have a speech prepared because I already knew exactly what I was about to say. "Jermaine Nazier Williams, I want you to know that I've loved you since day one. You are my rock, and next to God, you're my everything. You complete me, and I would rather die than spend another day without you. I look forward to growing old with you and—"

I was stopped dead in the middle of my vows when the room doors blew open. "Lovely Brown, get down on the ground!" one of the cops that had just bum-rushed the room said, and I froze. "Don't give me a reason!" he said with his gun pointed at me, and I did as I was told.

"What did I do?" I asked as I was being handcuffed.

"Officer, please don't! It's our wedding day!" Maine yelled, more like a plea.

When they raised me up off the ground, I saw the helpless look on his face, and I began to cry hysterically because I knew I would never become his wife or have his children. I knew I would never get to keep my promise to Shawnie or have Nichols over for dinner. I knew this because Meechie had already warned me: *"You are going down. I already put Plan B in motion."* His words echoed in my head.

"Well, well, well, Lovely. We meet again, and this time ain't shit you can do about it!" Vilan sang as he waved two large evidence bags in my face. "Recognize your gun from the motel shootout?"

he asked, putting it in my face with the engraving staring right back at me. "What about this?" he said, waving the bag with the ski mask and bloody clothes I wore the night of the truck robbery. He laughed, and I cried. Like I said in the beginning, if it wasn't for bad luck, a bitch wouldn't have any!

THE END

Trap House is an unflinching account of the goings on of an Atlanta drug den and the lives of those who frequent it. Its cast of characters include the Notorious P.I.G., the proprietor of the house, who uses his power to satisfy his licentious fetishes. Of his customers, there's Wanda, an exotic dancer who loathes P.I.G., but only tolerates him because he has the best dope in town. Wanda's boyfriend Mike is the owner of an upscale strip club, as well as a full time pimp.

Tiffany and Marcus are the teenage couple who began frequenting the Trap House after snorting a few lines at a party. Can their love for each other withstand the demands of their fledging addiction, or will it tear them apart?

P.I.G.'s wife Blast, doorman Earl and a host of other colorful characters round out the inhabitants of the Trap House.

Trap House is the bastard child of real life and the author's vivid imagination. Its author, Sa'id Salaam, paints a graphic portrait of the inner-workings of an under-world. He takes you so close you can almost hear the sizzle of the cocaine as it's smoked—almost smell the putrid aroma of crack as it's exhaled. Yet for all the grit and grime, Trap House has the audacity to be a love story. Through the sordid sex and brutality is an underlying tale of redemption and self empowerment. Trap House drives home the reality that everyone is a slave to something.

Who's your master?

Mz. Robinson

www.gstreetchronicles.com

5 STAR REVIEWS!!!

WELCOME TO THE JUNGLE!!

The King, raised in the hood with his family, saw a lot of suffering. He witnessed death and destruction within his own family—poverty and desperation of his own people. Instead of being part of the problem, he became part of the solution and rose to the top of his game. In his mind…it was survival.

After an encounter with a brilliant scientist, King began to plot something so huge, that no one would see it coming or be able to stop the cycle…not even the police.

www.gstreetchronicles.com

5 STAR REVIEWS!!!

Lies, deceit and murder ran rampant throughout the city of Atlanta. Real and his lady, Constance, were living in the lap of luxury, with fancy cars, expensive clothes and a million dollar home until someone close to them alerted the feds to their illegal activity.

At the blink of an eye their perfect life was turned upside down. Just as Real was sorting things out on the home front, the head of Miami's most powerful Cartel gave him an ultimatum that would eventually force him back into the life he had swore off forever. Knowing this lifestyle would surely put Constance in danger, he made plans to send her away until the score was settled but things spiraled out of control. Now Real and Constance are in a fight for survival where friends become enemies and murder is essential. Atlanta's underworld to Miami's most affluent community—no stone was left unturned as Real fought to keep Constance safe while attempting to regain control of the lifestyle he once would kill for.

From the city of Atlanta to the cell block of Georgia's most dangerous prison, life under the City Lights would never be the same.

Coming Soon!
Sabrina A. Eubanks
author of Karma I, II & III

Chase Brown has it all…he's wealthy, owns three of the hottest night clubs in New York City and he's boyishly handsome. Chase's rise to the top hasn't been easy and memories of his mother's murder, as she died in his arms when he was only twelve years old, still haunt him. These memories birth Smoke, his monstrous alter ego, who is psychotic and very dangerous.

Chase and his younger brother Corey are close—so close that his older brother, Cyrus, uses emotional blackmail to make Chase carry out his deceitful and murderous deeds. While attempting to bury Smoke and break free from his brother's spell, Chase meets the beautiful Bliss Riley. They fall madly in love but there is only one problem…Bliss isn't aware of Chase's murderous appetite and the demon that lives inside of the man she loves.

Will Chase be able to bury his demons for good and live happily ever after with the woman of his dreams or will Smoke take Chase and Bliss on a journey that will leave dead bodies throughout the city of New York? Only time will tell!

www.gstreetchronicles.com

Other good reads from G Street Chronicles

A-Town Veteran
Two Face
Dealt the Wrong Hand
Blocked In
Family Ties
Drama

Coming Soon!

The Lies We Tell for Love
Rapper's D-Lite
69
Lights Out
Drama II

Check out our Short Story Ebook Line

Gangsta Girl Mini Short Story Series
Lady Boss
Chronicles of a Junky

Name: ______________________________

Address: ______________________________

City/State: ______________________________

Zip: ______________________________

ALL BOOKS ARE $10 EACH

QTY	TITLE	PRICE
	Still Deceiving	
	Trap House	
	City Lights	
	A-Town Veteran	
	Beastmode	
	Executive Mistress	
	Essence of a Bad Girl	
	Dope, Death and Deception	
	Dealt the Wrong Hand	
	Married to His Lies	
	What We Won't Do for Love	
	Two Face	
	Family Ties	
	Blocked In	
	Drama	
	Shipping & Handling ($4 per book)	

TOTAL $ __________

To order online visit

www.gstreetchronicles.com

Send cashiers check or money order to:

G Street Chronicles

P.O. Box 490082 College Park, GA 30349